THE
SEVENTH
MOST
IMPORTANT
THING

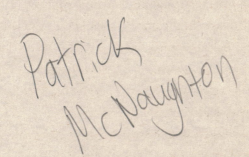

ALSO BY SHELLEY PEARSALL

THE SEVENTH MOST IMPORTANT THING

Shelley Pearsall

FP
PEA

A YEARLING BOOK

Text copyright © 2015 by Shelley Pearsall
Cover art copyright © 2015 by Karin Åkesson

All rights reserved. Published in the United States by Yearling, an imprint of
Random House Children's Books, a division of Penguin Random House LLC,
New York. Originally published in hardcover in the United States by Alfred A. Knopf,
an imprint of Random House Children's Books, New York, in 2015.

Yearling and the jumping horse design are registered trademarks of
Penguin Random House LLC.

Visit us on the Web! randomhousekids.com

Educators and librarians, for a variety of teaching tools, visit us at
RHTeachersLibrarians.com

The Library of Congress has cataloged the hardcover edition of this work as follows:
Pearsall, Shelley. The seventh most important thing / Shelley Pearsall.
pages cm.
Summary: "In 1963, thirteen-year-old Arthur is sentenced to community service
helping the neighborhood Junk Man after he throws a brick at the old man's head in a
moment of rage, but the junk he collects might be more important than he suspects.
Inspired by the work of American folk artist James Hampton." —Provided by publisher
ISBN 978-0-553-49728-1 (trade) — ISBN 978-0-553-49729-8 (lib. bdg.) —
ISBN 978-0-553-49730-4 (ebook)
1. Hampton, James, 1909–1964—Juvenile fiction. [1. Hampton, James, 1909–1964—Fiction.
2. Artists—Fiction. 3. Folk art—Fiction. 4. African Americans—Fiction. 5. Community
service (Punishment)—Fiction.] I. Title.
PZ7.P3166Se 2015
[Fic]—dc23
2014047761

ISBN 978-0-553-49731-1 (pbk.)

Printed in the United States of America

20 19 18 17 16 15 14 13 12 11

First Yearling Edition 2016

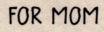
FOR MOM

ONE

On a bitter November day in Washington, D.C., when everything felt metallic—when the sky was gray and the wind stung and the dry leaves were making death-rattle sounds in the alleys—thirteen-year-old Arthur Owens picked up a brick from the corner of a crumbling building and threw it at an old man's head.

It wasn't an accident. The brick didn't topple off the decrepit building. It didn't fall from the heavens. Arthur Owens grabbed the brick with his own hands. He held it for a minute, noticing the cold weight of it—and then he raised his arm and flung it at the old trash picker known as the Junk Man, who was pushing a rusty grocery cart down the street.

Lucky for Arthur Owens, it was a windy day and his ability to see things at a distance had never been good. Also, the front wheel of the grocery cart wobbled off the sidewalk at precisely the right moment. As the old man leaned to straighten the cart, Arthur's brick slammed into his shoulder, sending him crumpling to the ground and the grocery cart skidding into the street.

If it hadn't been for the wind and the wobbly cart and Arthur's bad aim, it could have been a lot worse, everybody said. In the hospital later, the Junk Man told a newspaper reporter he believed it was an act of God.

"You being saved?" the reporter asked, already jotting down the answer he expected to hear.

"No" was the Junk Man's odd reply. "Me being hit."

Those were the facts. On November 9, 1963, the story ran in all three of the city's newspapers. One headline read: *THIRTEEN-YEAR-OLD BOY ATTACKS CITY MAN.* Then, in smaller type below, it said: *Man Saved by Good Samaritan.*

Most people didn't care much about the facts, though. They didn't care about the particular place where the crime happened—not a bad neighborhood, but not a good one either. Or how a newspaper delivery truck driver who'd taken a wrong turn spotted the injured man on the sidewalk and rushed him to a nearby hospital.

What everybody wanted to know was why.

Arthur Owens spent three weeks in the Juvenile Detention Home, better known as juvie, asking himself the same question.

TWO

A lot happened during the three weeks Arthur was locked up—the worst being that President Kennedy was killed. Then the guy who killed President Kennedy was killed. And then the Thanksgiving holiday passed by without much mention in juvie or anywhere else. Arthur didn't mind missing it. Along with the rest of the world, he didn't have much to be thankful for.

Four days after Thanksgiving, Arthur was brought to the courthouse for the hearing that would decide his fate. He was seated in a long row of bad kids, so he figured it was going to be a while.

Unfortunately, the judge assigned to hear Arthur Owens's case was not a listening sort of man. Judge Philip Warner liked his billowy black robe and the sound of his own voice too much. He reminded Arthur of those big horseflies that get stuck in your window in the summertime and buzz like mad and won't quit no matter what you do.

As the morning dragged on, the temperature in the courtroom rose. If Arthur had ever wondered what the fires of hell were like, Judge Warner's courtroom was giving him a pretty good idea. People who had come in wearing their winter coats and wool suit jackets were down to their shirt-sleeves.

Arthur kept his suit jacket neatly buttoned and his sleeves down. He knew it was what his mom would want.

Doing his best to stay awake, he tried to focus on the walls of the courtroom, which were covered with vertical panels of grooved wood. Arthur thought maybe the design was supposed to make the room appear sleek and modern, but the longer he stared at the panels, the more they seemed to ripple in sickening waves. He began to believe that even the walls had been designed as a kind of punishment.

The combination of all these things—the swimming walls, the heat, the sweat, and the judge's endless voice—made him feel as if he just might puke when his turn finally came.

"Arthur T. Owens, approach the bench," the bailiff called out.

It was only a few steps from his chair to the judge's bench, but to Arthur it felt like miles. He could sense the breathing, sweaty mass of people behind him the way you sense the weight of bullies right before they're about to smash you into a wall of lockers at school.

There had been a lot of bullies in juvie—it was practically a bully vacation spot.

4

No doubt some of the people in the courtroom were surprised to see what Arthur Owens looked like as he walked to the front. He wasn't your typical juvie thug. He didn't have meat slabs for hands, or full facial hair, or an insolent grin.

He thought he could hear a few whispers behind him. "That's him?"

Arthur Owens was slender, pale, and moody-looking. Maybe he was a little taller than some thirteen-year-olds—his father had been tall—but mostly, he was someone who wouldn't get noticed walking down the street. When his brown hair flopped over his eyes, Arthur had the bad habit of leaving it there, which drove his mother crazy. He also didn't smile much.

As Arthur glanced nervously at the long row of juvenile delinquents, he could tell he was one of the youngest of all the young criminals waiting on the judge that day. And from what he could see, he was the only person who was wearing an almost-new funeral suit that didn't fit him very well.

THREE

Judge Warner took a moment to study Arthur Owens when he reached the bench. It was his way of making the kids squirm.

As the judge glared at him, Arthur tried to decide what to do with his hands and feet, which suddenly seemed to be completely useless objects. He crossed and uncrossed his arms, shifted from one foot to the other, and did his best to ignore the sickening flip-flopping in his stomach. Sweat made his undershirt stick to his back.

The judge finally spoke after glancing down at a piece of paper handed to him by the bailiff. "You are Arthur Thomas Owens?"

"Yes," Arthur thought he said.

"I didn't hear you, young man."

"Yes, Your Honor," Arthur replied, slightly louder.

"Look up at me when you are speaking."

Arthur swallowed. He hated looking at people when he was speaking. It made him feel like they could X-ray every thought in his head. Usually, he had his hair to hide behind, but that morning his mother had taken a pair of scissors to the front of it. "To make you look less guilty," she'd told him.

Arthur didn't think his hair had anything to do with his guilt, but there was nothing left now but a jagged fringe high above his forehead. He tugged at it with his fingers.

"Okay," he mumbled, glancing up at the judge's thick round glasses and oddly magnified eyes, then looking back down at his feet. There was a long pause, as if the judge was trying to decide if he was entitled to more respect than he was getting. The room was quiet, expectant.

When the judge's gaze finally returned to the paper in his hands, Arthur held back a loud sigh of relief.

"According to what I've read about your case, I understand you attacked a man named James Hampton in a vicious and unprovoked manner on November eighth. Is that correct, Mr. Owens?"

Arthur blinked, momentarily confused by the name.

James Hampton? Who was James Hampton?

It took him a minute to figure out the judge was talking about the old Junk Man. Arthur tried not to look surprised by the fact that the man had a real name.

Everybody had a name, of course, but he had to admit he'd never thought about the Junk Man having one. He couldn't recall anybody in the neighborhood ever using it—especially not a name as formal-sounding as James Hampton, which could have belonged to a school principal or somebody's grandfather.

It definitely didn't make Arthur feel any better about what he'd done.

It also didn't make him feel better to find out that the Junk Man—James Hampton—had come to court that day to watch what happened. He was seated in the crowd only a few rows back from where Arthur stood.

The judge pointed him out. A shocked breath caught in Arthur's throat.

He didn't even look like the same person.

The Junk Man's gray-white hair, usually disheveled, was now close-cut and carefully trimmed. He wasn't wearing his familiar raggedy clothes and foggy eyeglasses either. Instead, he had on a neatly pressed brown suit and striped orange tie. Somehow he appeared taller. And less crazy.

But you couldn't miss the heavy white cast covering one arm and the sling of fabric that formed a triangle, almost like the letter *A* for Arthur, across the old man's chest.

Arthur swallowed hard, staring at the cast, staring at what he'd done. The *A* seemed to get more visible, more accusing, the longer he stared at it.

"Mr. Owens, I'll repeat my question. Are you the one who attacked Mr. Hampton?"

"Yes, sir," Arthur whispered.

"Then I want you to look at this innocent man you injured—and, quite frankly, could have killed," the judge continued.

There was a murmur of outraged agreement in the courtroom.

"And I want you to tell me what was going through your mind that afternoon," said the judge, his voice rising. He was proud of his intimidating, kid-shaking baritone. "I want to know exactly what could have compelled you to throw a brick at Mr. Hampton as he was minding his own business walking down the street."

Arthur was silent. He looked at his feet. The too-long funeral pants made pools of black fabric over his polished shoes. He noticed how the orange carpet below them was nearly the same shade as the Junk Man's tie. He wondered if he'd be sentenced to jail for life if he refused to give a reason for what he'd done.

"Did you attack Mr. Hampton because he looked like a helpless old man—pardon my choice of words," the judge added apologetically, glancing in the direction of the Junk Man. "Did he seem like an easy target to you?"

"No, sir," Arthur heard himself answer reluctantly.

"Were you attempting to rob him?"

Arthur shook his head. *Robbing the Junk Man* would have been an almost-funny statement in any other place, but he didn't dare laugh, not even inside his own head.

"Was it his color that caused you to attack him?"

Color? Confused, Arthur turned to look at the Junk Man

again, not sure what color the judge was referring to. Was he talking about the white cast? The orange tie?

The judge grew more impatient. "I am asking you, young man—and this is a very serious question—did you throw the brick at him because he is a black man?"

What? Arthur's stomach gave a sickening lurch. This was a possibility he'd never thought about. Never in a million years considered. He could feel his heart thudding wildly, his mind racing. The Junk Man wasn't a color. He was just the Junk Man.

But the man's skin was light brown. That was a fact.

And Arthur's was peeled-onion white. That was a fact too.

He'd just never put those two facts together.

Arthur knew people's race wasn't something you messed around with. There were marches and protests about it on television all the time—and Arthur didn't even pay much attention to the news. Could the judge truly believe he'd been trying to stir up some kind of trouble by hitting the Junk Man?

Although he had sworn to himself that he would say nothing—that he would never talk about what had made him so angry on that November afternoon—Arthur had no choice. His father wouldn't have wanted him to stay silent and be accused of something far worse.

So Arthur licked his dry lips and spoke.

"Your Honor," he said, trying to keep his voice from shaking. "It wasn't his color."

The judge's reply was icy. "Then what was it?"

Arthur knew the answer would sound crazy to everyone in the room. He knew no one would understand, and it would probably earn him a permanent bunk in juvie with nothing but olive-green clothes and bad food and lukewarm showers for the rest of his life.

Looking down at the floor, Arthur said in a barely audible voice, "It was because of his hat, Your Honor."

While this might have seemed like a smart-aleck answer to the judge, to the courtroom, and to anyone who heard it, it was, in fact, the truth. Arthur had thrown the brick because of a hat.

FOUR

The hat in question had been missing from the hall closet, along with everything else that had belonged to his father, when Arthur got home from school that November day. It was November 8, just as the judge had said. A Friday.

Arthur remembered opening the closet to hang up his stuff. He'd just taken off his coat and tossed his shoes inside when he realized something was different. The closet was tidy and half empty. It smelled like Murphy's oil soap.

With his heart hammering in his chest, he began pushing through the coats that were left, searching for his father's old corduroy jacket. It was a big, faded coat that held the shape of his father's shoulders and smelled of stale cigarette smoke and beer and motor oil, as if he'd just taken it off after getting home from work. (Arthur still liked to imagine that he had.)

Nothing.

Arthur's eyes darted toward the row of hat pegs, looking for the motorcycle cap that had belonged to his father. It was one of those slick Harley-Davidson caps—black leather with a silver chain and the orange-winged logo on the brim.

If you wanted to find Tom Owens in a crowd, all you had to do was look for that cap, sitting slightly to one side—never straight, always jaunty. He was wearing it in nearly every picture the family had of him.

But except for the one with his little sister's pink knit hat, all of the pegs were empty.

Feeling more and more uneasy, Arthur pounded up the stairs to his parents' room, making the walls of the small house shake. He and his sister shared one room at the top of the stairs. His parents shared the other. Both rooms were shabby. Arthur's family had never had a lot of money.

The door to his parents' room stood open. Arthur saw that the old radio his dad used to listen to ball games on was missing. The wedding picture that had always been on his parents' wall was gone. Even the ashtray on the windowsill—the one he'd made for his dad in art class in third grade, a hideous green-and-blue swirl of clay—wasn't there.

Arthur had been afraid this was coming. It had been three months since his dad died, although it still felt like yesterday.

Arthur hadn't forgotten how upset his mom had been after the funeral, how she'd gone through the kitchen like a bulldozer when they got home.

"I don't want anything that reminds me of Tom left in this house! Nothing! Not one damn thing!" she'd shouted, half crying, half yelling, as she threw out everything she could find in the refrigerator and cupboards: His father's booze. Bags of corn chips. Packs of cigarettes. Cans of pork and beans. Anything that had belonged to him. Anything he'd liked.

Only Arthur's begging and his sister's tears had finally stopped her from clearing out even more that night.

And now the rest of his father's things were gone.

For the past couple of weeks, his mom had been hinting that it was time for them to move on. "We need to make a new start," she'd been saying.

But he never thought she would do something like this without giving him some warning. Had she just packed up his dad's stuff and thrown everything out while he was at school?

Feeling sick, he pounded back down the stairs, yanked on his shoes, and ran outside to look.

Up and down the street, the curbs were lined with empty metal garbage cans. Some of the lids were already rolling away in the gusty November wind. Leftover bits of trash stuck to the city street.

Arthur began to sprint, careening madly down his block and around the corner, as if he could somehow catch the garbage truck and save his father.

That was when he noticed the old man who often came through the neighborhood on trash day with his grocery cart, looking for junk. "Got any shiny stuff for me today?" he'd holler if people were outside. "Anything valuable you don't want?"

Everybody called him the Junk Man. They knew he picked through their garbage whether they let him or not. He'd been collecting junk for years—as far back as Arthur could remember. Always pushing the same rusty cart down the street, and always wearing the same filthy tan coat, summer or winter.

Arthur had seen the guy take wine bottles out of the trash and put them straight into his coat pockets. Or sometimes he'd haul away people's discarded furniture—broken chairs, headboards, small tables—in a teetering pile in his cart. One person even spotted him sitting on a piano bench in their yard once, playing an invisible piano.

He was a crazy old drunk, people said.

Which was why, when Arthur saw his father's motorcycle cap perched crookedly on the Junk Man's head, he completely lost it. He knew the Junk Man had stolen it from them. He knew the worthless trash picker had gone through their garbage, piece by piece, and picked out the best things of his father's to take with him.

And in that moment, all of the fury that had been building inside Arthur since his father's death came exploding out.

It was bad enough that his mother had thrown away his father's things without even asking him. Bad enough that most people thought his father had thrown away his life and didn't deserve to be remembered. Bad enough that other kids had their fathers and his dad was dead.

But when Arthur saw the crazy Junk Man wearing the most important thing of all to his dad . . . that was the final straw. Did the old man think it was okay to steal things from dead people? Did he wander around the neighborhood waiting for people to die so he could run off with their favorite possessions? Was that what he did? Or was he mocking Arthur's dad by wearing his hat? Was it some kind of sick joke?

Arthur knew his mind wasn't thinking straight, but he couldn't control it. It was like a runaway train, racing faster and faster toward a wall.

He saw the pile of crumbled bricks next to a closed-down building on the street corner. He picked up one. It was the only thing he could think of doing. He would punish the old man for what he'd done. He would punish death for what it had done. He would punish everybody.

The brick felt cold and rough in his hand. It was a dangerous thing to be holding—he recognized that much. A small voice in the back of Arthur's mind tried to tell him to stop, to think about what he was doing.

Arthur told the voice to go to hell.

And then he raised his arm and threw.

FIVE

If it had been up to the judge, he would have thrown the book at Arthur T. Owens. He didn't believe a word of the boy's story.

"So I think seeing him wearing my dad's hat was what made me, you know, do what I did," Arthur said, finishing his stumbling explanation.

Right. The judge didn't buy it. In his opinion, the boy was just using his father's death as an excuse for causing trouble.

All you had to do was look at the facts in the kid's paperwork: Arthur had a father who'd dropped out of school, who'd been in jail a couple of times for minor crimes, and who'd died drunk. What were the chances his son would turn out any different? He was already heading down the same path.

"In my experience, the apple doesn't fall far from the tree," the judge said to Arthur.

But James Hampton didn't see it that way.

After Arthur and the judge finished talking, Mr. Hampton stood up and asked the bailiff if he could have a quick word with the judge. The bailiff asked if it could wait, and James Hampton said as politely as an army soldier, "No, sir, with all due respect, it can't."

Arthur was still having a hard time believing the Junk Man and James Hampton were the same person. He kept wondering if it was some kind of trick, if maybe the guy was an actor or something.

The two men—James Hampton and the judge—stepped out of the room, and the "quick word" stretched into an hour. The courtroom was dismissed for lunch.

Although he wasn't the least bit hungry, Arthur sat in the courthouse hallway with his mother and ate the baloney and cheese sandwich she had brought for him. It tasted like baloney-flavored cardboard, but he didn't want his mom to start crying again if he turned it down.

She looked like she'd been crying for a year. Usually, his mom's makeup was perfect, and her dark hair never changed. It was always styled with the same big, glossy waves held in place with the same white velvet headband.

But now her face was puffy and splotched with red. She kept twisting a pink tissue in her fingers, until it fell into shreds on the black dress she was wearing. Pretty soon, she looked as if she was covered in melting pink snow-flakes.

Arthur wasn't sure why his mother had worn her funeral

dress to court that day. Was she already expecting the worst? He'd had to wear his funeral suit because it was the only suit he owned.

"I'm sorry, Mom," Arthur said for the thousandth time.

He'd said it every day she'd come to visit him in juvie. He'd put it at the bottom of every letter he'd written to her. He'd repeated it that morning when she'd brought the suit for him to wear.

"You should have let me know something was wrong," his mother replied for the thousandth time. "Your sister lost a tooth and got an A in reading this week. Did I tell you that already?" she asked, her eyes spilling over with tears again. Sometimes when Arthur's mom was upset, she didn't make much sense.

"No, you didn't," Arthur replied, even though she had already told him. Twice.

"Do you think they'll ever let you come home again?"

Arthur sighed. "I don't know, Mom."

But he didn't think the chances were very good.

When court resumed after lunch, Arthur was called to the front. He figured he was doomed when the judge said, "This is a highly unconventional sentence, young man," before he had reached the judge's bench.

Earlier that day, Arthur had seen kids who had stolen a few lousy bags of chips and candy get sent back to juvie for sixty days or more by Judge Warner. Everybody said he was one of the toughest judges around. So Arthur knew something "unconventional" had to be pretty bad.

"In other words," the judge continued sternly, glaring at Arthur, "it is not the punishment I would have chosen for you."

It wasn't hard to imagine the various punishments the judge might have chosen. Arthur had already pictured all of them.

The judge glanced toward the Junk Man, who had returned to his seat in the third row and was sitting with his hands folded in his lap. "However, Mr. Hampton has made it clear to me that he is not interested in retribution, but in redemption." He looked at Arthur. "Do you know what *redemption* means?"

Arthur thought it might have something to do with church, but he was pretty sure the judge wasn't allowed to sentence people to go to church.

He shook his head.

"Well, you ought to know. Look it up later. *Re-demption.*" The judge gestured impatiently at the courtroom. "I don't have time to be everybody's schoolteacher here. As you can see," he continued, pointing toward the Junk Man, "you have left Mr. Hampton unable to do his work as a result of his injuries, so he has offered an unusual proposal for me to consider."

The judge fixed his gaze on Arthur. "Instead of sentencing you to the Juvenile Detention Home for an *exceedingly* long time—which I won't hesitate to do if I ever see you in my courtroom again—Mr. Hampton has requested that you be assigned to work for him until his arm has healed."

The courtroom behind Arthur buzzed with confusion. What had the judge just said? The brick-throwing kid was being sentenced to work for the guy *he'd tried to kill*? Had Judge Warner completely lost his mind?

Arthur stared at the judge, as confused and startled as everyone else. Work for the Junk Man? What could the judge possibly be thinking?

In spite of himself, Arthur spoke up. He made sure to use the Junk Man's real name, although it still seemed strangely unreal to him. "What sort of work does Mr. Hampton do, sir?"

The judge arched his eyebrows. "You don't know?"

"I'm not sure," Arthur mumbled. He couldn't imagine any judge would knowingly sentence a kid to dig through people's garbage looking for wine bottles and busted-up furniture. Did the old man have another job nobody knew about?

The judge smiled in a rather smug way. "Well, I guess you'll soon find out, won't you, Mr. Owens?"

And with that, Arthur Owens was allowed to go home.

SIX

Going home was the best part of Arthur's sentence. He decided he'd worry about the other parts later. Anything was better than a ride back to juvie in the grim gray school bus with bars on the windows and a driver with a gun.

For once, he didn't mind having to kick his sister's pile of stuffed animals out of the way when he walked into their bedroom. At least he had a bedroom he could walk into.

The frosting-pink bedspread on Barbara's side of the room didn't bug him nearly as much as it usually did either. He didn't even care that his sister had left a large crayon picture on his bed showing Barbara, frowning, with the words *Don't Do Any More Bad Things, Arthur* underneath it.

He was just glad to be home.

• • •

"We need to have a talk," his mom said, sticking her head into the bedroom before he'd had time to unpack or get changed.

"Now?" Arthur sighed. Couldn't he have five minutes to himself?

"I don't want to let it wait."

His mom was like that. Whenever she had something on her mind, she had to talk about it right then. Arthur was the exact opposite. He could hold things inside forever.

They sat on the saggy bed in his mom's room, which still felt empty with all of his dad's things gone. Although the door was half closed, Arthur could tell his little sister was sitting right outside. He could hear her fidgety feet on the stairway.

"We're going to have some new rules now that you're home," his mom said. She pulled a folded piece of notepaper from the pocket of her funeral dress. "I've written them down."

"Rules?" Arthur was surprised, because his mom had never been very strict.

Arthur's mom glanced down at her paper. "First rule. You are going to talk to me more when you are upset. I mean that, Artie." She looked at Arthur, her mascara still smudged from the day in court. "You have to talk to me more about how you're feeling and not just hold it inside. I don't want to go through this again." He could see her eyes starting to tear up.

"Fine. Okay. I will," he said, trying to get his mom to

move on to another topic. He didn't want to keep going over why he'd thrown the brick.

"Second, no more getting into trouble with the police. That's how your dad started when he was younger. Getting into fights at school or street racing or whatever else he did back then."

He glared at his mom. "I'm not like that."

It kind of made Arthur mad that she would say this to him, but deep down, he couldn't help wondering if she was right. His middle name, Thomas, was from his dad, but that didn't mean they were the same people. Or did it? Until he threw the brick, Arthur had never been in trouble with the cops before.

"Well, I just want to make sure," his mom said in a not-very-convincing voice. She looked down at her paper again. "Third, you will come straight home every day after school to watch Barbara."

"Okay." Arthur wasn't really sure why this was a new rule. He'd always watched Barbara.

His mom folded up the paper and stuck it back in her dress pocket. "Last, and this is hard for me to say . . ." His mom's voice shook a little. "We have a lot of bills right now. Until I find a new job, things are pretty tight, okay?" Arthur knew his mom was working a couple of waitressing jobs to make ends meet. He also knew that some of their money problems were due to him, since the court had said they had to pay the Junk Man's hospital bills.

"That's it." She reached out and gave him a hug. She

smelled like soap and hair spray. "I love you and I'm glad you're home."

"I'm glad to be home too," Arthur said awkwardly, feeling embarrassed.

It felt like he'd been away for months.

SEVEN

"Were you scared?" Barbara asked, sucking on a grape lollipop as she watched Arthur unpack his paper bag of clothes later.

The small paper bag was all he'd been allowed to bring when the cops had arrested him for throwing the brick after somebody had seen him running back home. You could take one toothbrush, one comb, and one set of street clothes to wear when you left juvie. That was it. In juvie, everybody wore the same olive-green jumpsuits. If you were lucky, the previous owner hadn't died in them.

Arthur shrugged. "No, I wasn't scared. Not really."

"Did everybody in the jail have guns?"

"I wasn't in jail."

"Mom said you were."

"Well, I wasn't."

Carefully, Arthur put his clothes in the two top drawers of the dresser he shared with his sister. It was odd how grateful he was for everything all of a sudden: The beat-up old dresser with Barbara's Winnie the Pooh stickers on it. The clothes he hadn't seen in three weeks. His sister. The disgusting smell of her grape lollipop.

"Was it a school for bad kids?"

"Kind of."

"Did you make any friends there?" Barbara stopped partway through licking her lollipop, as if this scary possibility had just occurred to her.

Arthur had to stifle a sarcastic laugh. "No."

There were no friends in juvie, he thought. Just varying degrees of people you didn't want to have as enemies.

Arthur's bunkmate had been a huge kid called Slash. On Arthur's first day there, Slash had held a rusty razor to his neck and told him that if he farted, belched, barfed, or breathed too loudly in bed—Arthur was on the top bunk—he was dead.

Fortunately, Slash had turned out to be the loudest snorer in the room, so Arthur still had a head attached to his shoulders, even if he hadn't gotten much sleep.

"You know, I can help you make better friends if you want," Barbara said. "I have lots of them at school." She began going through a long list of names on her fingers.

"Okay. Thanks." Arthur forced himself to smile at his sister. Despite everything that had happened, somehow she was the only one in the family who seemed to have stayed fairly okay. Normal. And right now, he didn't mind sharing a room with a normal kid, even if she was a curly-haired seven-year-old who played with Barbies. At least her name wasn't Slash.

That night, after Arthur crawled into his bed, he was surprised when his little sister whispered from the darkness on her side of the room, "You awake, Arthur?" She'd gone to bed hours before him.

"It's late. Aren't you supposed to be asleep?" he replied, trying to sound big-brotherly. It was past eleven.

"Yes, but I can't."

"Well, try." Arthur turned to face the wall and tugged the covers over his shoulders, as if the conversation was finished.

"Are you going to die, Arthur?"

Arthur's head snapped back toward his sister's side of the room. *"What?"*

"Some of my friends said Daddy died because he was bad and drank too much and went too fast and crashed his motorcycle, and now you've been bad and you had to go to jail, so are you going to die too?"

"Don't be stupid, Barbara," Arthur blurted out. "I wasn't in jail. I'm not going to die. Just be quiet and go to sleep, will you?"

Arthur knew he should have been more understanding. His sister was only a little kid trying to get some answers.

There was a long silence. Now Arthur couldn't sleep. His bed felt too soft. The room seemed too weirdly quiet after juvie. Barbara had started him thinking about death and his dad.

Then Barbara spoke up again—almost a whisper.

"Do you think Daddy's in heaven?"

Arthur gave an aggravated sigh. "Of course he is. Where else do you think he'd be? God, you're driving me nuts with your questions tonight, Barbara. I'm tired and I want to go to sleep, so just shut up and stop talking, okay?" He smacked his pillow and turned toward the wall again. Thankfully, Barbara seemed to get the message this time.

But the truth was, Arthur wasn't sure. About heaven or anything else. He had a lot of doubts. The doubts often kept him awake. Sometimes they gave him nightmares. He could see the cops at their door, with little drops of rain glistening like glass on their shoulders, saying the word *instantly* again and again. His father had died *instantly*.

He remembered overhearing one of his aunts talking at the funeral home, saying how it was too bad her brother—Arthur's dad—hadn't been more of a religious person in life because heaven was such a beautiful place for believers to spend eternity.

She never did say where she thought everybody else went.

After about fifteen minutes of lying there in the darkness, thinking about heaven and his dad and the word *instantly* and how he probably shouldn't have been so mean to Barbara the first night he was home, he threw off the covers and got out of bed.

He had just reached the door when Barbara whispered, "Where are you going?"

"To get a book downstairs."

"Why?"

"To look up something. Go to sleep," he said firmly, shutting the door behind him.

His mother's bedroom door was already closed. He padded softly down the steps to the small bookshelf in the living room—the one that was stuffed with mail and bills. Somewhere on the shelves was a dictionary, he remembered. His mother's high school name, Linda Wesley, was on the inside. That was how old it was.

He turned to the word he was looking for:

redemption (ri-demp'-shun) *n*. 1. The act of being rescued or set free. 2. The act of being saved from consequences. 3. The payment of an obligation. 4. Salvation from sin.

If he was supposed to understand what *redemption* meant after reading the definitions, he didn't. How could the judge think working for the Junk Man would rescue him and set him free? What did "the payment of an obligation" mean? And what consequences, other than juvie, was he being saved from?

None of it made any sense. Irritated, he pushed the dictionary onto the shelf and went back to bed.

The next morning, when he walked outside to get the newspaper for his mother, he found something else he didn't understand.

At first he thought there was a deflated balloon on the

porch steps. Then he realized, no—it was a hat. A black leather motorcycle cap missing the orange Harley-Davidson wings on its brim.

Arthur's heart pounded as he picked it up. It was his father's old hat, he was almost certain. Underneath the cap was a note scrawled on a scrap of cardboard:

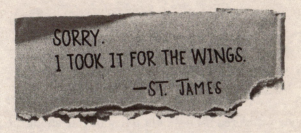

Arthur looked up and down his street, which was empty. He had no idea what to think.

EIGHT

Arthur wondered if he should tell someone about the note, especially the weird part about the wings and St. James. Had the Junk Man left it for him? And if so, why had he signed it St. James?

He considered bringing the note to his probation officer when he went for his first appointment a few days later, but after meeting her, he was glad he hadn't. In juvie, he'd heard that some officers were nice and some were complete jerks. His officer turned out to be a short, box-shaped woman named Wanda Billie who didn't seem to have much patience for anything.

Her office was in the basement of the courthouse. Arthur's mother dropped him off while she went to look for free parking, and it took him forever to find the right hallway and the right numbered door. The whole place appeared to have been designed as a human maze.

"You're late," Officer Billie said when he walked into her office fifteen minutes past his two o'clock appointment time.

Arthur glanced at the clock above the officer's head and tried to explain. "I couldn't find—"

"*Stop.*" The officer held up her square-fingered hand. "Are you late or are you not late, Mr. Owens?"

"The elevator wasn't—"

"*Stop.*"

Already the hand thing was getting old. Arthur wondered if the lady had been a traffic cop in a previous life.

"Did I ask you what made you late?" The officer chomped on her gum.

"No, ma'am." Arthur shook his head.

"Have a seat." Officer Billie gestured to the cracked black plastic chair in front of her desk. Everything in the room appeared to be broken. The wall next to him had a spiderweb of cracks in it, as if someone had tried (and failed) to put their fist through it. He sat down gingerly on the broken chair. He kept his hands in his lap.

"So." Officer Billie leaned back in her chair. "You're the kid with the anger problems who threw a rock at a black man's head."

"Brick," Arthur tried to explain. "And it wasn't because—"

"*Stop.*" The officer put up her hand again. "I don't care about the details. All I care about is you, buddy. Right here. Right now." She leaned forward and rapped her knuckles on the desk. "How are you going to change your life?"

Arthur didn't answer, and he didn't think Officer Billie

was expecting an answer, because she pushed on without waiting for his reply.

"You understand you've been given a second chance, right? I'm in charge of overseeing your second chance." She pointed to her barrel-shaped self. "And you better not mess up. None of my kids ever messes up. Got that?"

Arthur nodded.

Putting on a pair of reading glasses, she picked up the single sheet of paper that was sitting in the middle of her desk. Arthur had never seen anybody with such an empty desk. He hoped he wasn't her only project.

"Now, it says here you'll be working four hours a week for Mr. Hampton until you complete the one hundred and twenty hours required by the court." The officer stopped reading and glared at Arthur over the top of her glasses. "That doesn't mean a hundred and eighteen hours or a hundred and nineteen and a half hours or a hundred and nineteen and three-quarters hours, got it? I don't care whether you get lost, sick, tired, or your dog dies. You are required to finish a hundred and twenty hours, no excuses."

Arthur managed to resist saying that he didn't have a dog. "What sort of work will I be doing?" he asked politely.

"Whatever you are told to do, buddy."

He knew he shouldn't keep going with this futile line of conversation, but he did. "I'm not sure the judge knows that sometimes . . ." He hesitated. "The Junk Man—well, Mr. Hampton—goes through people's garbage looking for stuff, so I just wanted to make sure that I'm not—"

"Stop." Officer Billie held up her hand. "Who is the one with the problem here?"

Arthur had to try very hard not to sigh out loud. "Me?"

"That's right. Did Mr. Hampton throw the brick?"

"No."

"Did Mr. Hampton get himself arrested and sent to the detention home?"

"No."

The officer jabbed her finger toward Arthur. "Then I don't think he's the one we should be worrying about here, do you?"

"No, probably not," Arthur mumbled. He stared at the scratched wooden top of the desk, wondering how many times he had to meet with Officer Billie. He hoped it wasn't very often.

As if she'd read his mind, the woman said, "Once a month. You come here once a month—next time, be on time—and we'll talk about how your assignment is progressing. Mr. Hampton will record your hours and report to me also. Then I report to the judge. The buck stops with me. That's it. Pretty simple. Got it?"

"Yes," Arthur replied, desperately hoping the meeting was over.

Officer Billie held a crisply folded piece of paper toward him. "Here's the address where you are to meet Mr. Hampton on Saturday for your first day of work. Be on time. Work hard. Four hours, no excuses, remember?"

Arthur took the paper and nodded. "Yes, ma'am." He stood up and started to ease toward the door.

"Stop," the officer called out behind him. Arthur didn't even need to look to know she had her hand up. He turned around reluctantly.

"Don't forget," she said, pointing a warning finger at him. "Don't mess up."

NINE

Arthur kept hearing Officer Billie's words in his head as he walked to James Hampton's house on the first Saturday in December. *Don't mess up.*

A miserable, pebbly white sleet was coming down from the colorless sky. Arthur had told his mom he wanted to walk. It was only a few blocks to the address on the paper, he'd insisted. Plus, he knew they didn't have the money to waste on gas.

Arthur wiped his cold and already-running nose on his sleeve. Stupidly, he hadn't thought to wear gloves or bring a hat. He'd just wanted to get out of the house that morning and get his first four hours over with. At least there would only be 116 more to go after that.

He had no clue what to expect. Would Mr. Hampton have him running errands or cleaning toilets or what? He wasn't even sure *who* to expect. The crazy Junk Man with the ragged tan coat and fogged eyeglasses? Or the polite, soft-spoken man in the brown tweed suit?

He pulled Officer Billie's paper out of his pocket and checked the address again. On the back of the same page, Arthur's mother had drawn a pretty lame map of how to get to Seventh Street, where he was supposed to go.

Arthur shook his head. It wasn't like he needed a map. His school bus drove past these neighborhoods every day, although he'd never actually walked around in them. At the next street, he had to make a left.

Arthur squinted at the numbers as he walked. Unlike his street, where the small bungalows and square yards were almost all the same, the houses on Seventh Street were old two-story ones, jammed together like mismatched puzzle pieces. Some had porches in front and leaning garages in the back. Others had only a narrow patch of yard with a gravel driveway between them.

Scattered along the street were some neighborhood businesses that looked as if they'd been there for years: A gas station on the corner. An auto repair shop with a couple of rusty cars in its side lot. A tattoo shop called Groovy Jim's Tattoos. And a small grocery store.

The only thing missing was the address he was trying to find.

Arthur walked up and down both sides of the street. There wasn't much traffic for a Saturday morning. A few city buses drove by without stopping. He folded and unfolded the paper in his pocket, checking it over and over again, until the ink was smeared and the sleet had turned the page into a soggy mess. He was freezing and losing time.

The closest address to the one on his page was the tattoo shop's. He remembered Officer Billie's warning: *No excuses. I don't care whether you get lost, sick, tired, or your dog dies.*

He decided to pull open the door of Groovy Jim's Tattoos.

A blast of warm air hit his face. The weird antiseptic smell of the place made his eyes water. He blinked, trying to see if anybody was around. Hawaiian-sounding ukulele music was playing somewhere. A black-and-white cat came over and rubbed against his ankles.

"Can I help you?"

All Arthur saw at first was a frizzy mop of hair behind the counter. Then the rest of the guy emerged from where he'd been sitting. There was no question this was Groovy Jim. Arthur didn't even have to ask. The guy wore a T-shirt with the words *Ban the Bomb* across the front. Green tattoos spiraled up his skinny white arms.

Reluctantly, Arthur pulled the scrap of paper out of his pocket, wishing he didn't have to look so stupid in front of a stranger. With the way his eyes were watering, he knew the guy was probably going to think he'd been crying.

"I'm trying to find this address," he mumbled, holding the page toward Groovy Jim. "You know where it is?"

The guy glanced at the paper briefly and handed it back to him. "So how long have you been looking?"

Arthur stretched the time only a little bit. "About an hour or two."

That was what it had felt like, anyhow.

The guy laughed. "That's all?"

Arthur couldn't tell if he was joking. When he didn't smile, Groovy Jim gave him an odd look. "Okay." He motioned toward a door at the back. "Follow me. I'll show you where it is, kiddo."

Arthur didn't really like being called kiddo, but he didn't think the guy meant it as an insult. Groovy Jim seemed like the kind of person who probably called everybody kiddo. Even the cat.

He also didn't appear to be in much of a hurry. He moved through his shop as if he was on a Sunday stroll in the park.

None of this was helping Arthur get his four hours started any sooner.

When they finally reached the back of the shop, it took Groovy Jim another few minutes to unlock and push open the metal door. A gust of cold air rushed in.

"The place you were trying to find is in the back. See the garage?" As he leaned against the heavy door to keep it open, Groovy Jim pointed to a small brick building standing by itself at the end of the gravel alley. "That's the place you're looking for."

A garage? Arthur balked. He hadn't expected a garage. Had he been given the wrong address? How was a garage somebody's house?

Groovy Jim glanced at him curiously, maybe wondering what was up. "You know Mr. Hampton, right?"

"Kind of," Arthur replied, tugging at the jagged front of

his hair uncertainly. He looked at the garage again, making sure it really was a garage. There were no front doors or windows or anything, were there?

"Does he live there?" he asked.

Groovy Jim shook his head. "Don't think so. He just comes here to work. I see him a lot in the evenings, carrying things in and out with his grocery cart. I guess he builds or fixes things or something back there."

"What kinds of things?"

Groovy Jim shrugged. "Don't know. Never asked." He waved a tattooed arm at the garage. "Go ahead and knock. If he's there, I'm sure he'll answer. He seems like a nice enough guy. But I gotta go back inside. I'm freezing out here, kiddo."

"Okay, thanks." Arthur forced a smile.

"Good luck."

The door closed behind Groovy Jim with a hard slam, and Arthur was left on his own in a swirl of spitting snow.

TEN

A garage. Arthur still had no idea what to do.

He wandered slowly down the gravel alleyway toward the building. It was your typical brick garage with one of those big corrugated metal doors. Someone had painted the address over the door, but they hadn't done a very good job of it. Long drips ran down the bricks, so the numbers almost looked as if they were melting. Since none of the address was visible from the street, Arthur wasn't sure why anybody had bothered.

On the far side of the garage, Arthur noticed another door. It had a real doorknob, at least, which gave him a little bit of hope. Maybe if he knocked on it . . .

As he stepped over broken bits of concrete and coils of rusted wire to reach the side door, he tried not to think about how dangerous all of this seemed: An out-of-the-way garage. A run-down neighborhood. Nobody around. He knew he should probably go back home and call Officer Billie or the judge or somebody.

But if he complained, it was possible—no, extremely likely—that they'd send him back to juvie. And which was worse: wandering around deserted alleys or having rusty razors held to your neck?

He knocked on the side door cautiously. Just a few knocks to see if anybody answered.

No one did.

He pounded on the door a little harder and tried the doorknob.

It didn't budge.

Feeling more irritated, he walked around to the front of the garage and banged his fist on the corrugated door—which turned out to be a really dumb idea, because the door was freezing cold and a lot more painful to hit than you'd think. He could hear the hollow thumps of his fist echoing inside the building. If James Hampton was working inside, he was either completely deaf or ignoring him.

Arthur didn't spot the grocery cart until he was about to give up and leave.

It was sitting at an odd angle, jutting out from the side of the garage nearest the street. As he stepped back from the corrugated door, he saw it out of the corner of his eye. He was pretty sure it was the same cart the Junk Man always used when he came through the neighborhood. The same one he'd been pushing when Arthur hit him.

There was something taped to the front of it. Arthur walked over to see what it was.

Just like the note he'd found underneath his father's hat a few days earlier, this message was written on a scrap of cardboard. It couldn't have been there long, because the cardboard was mostly dry and the ink hadn't smudged yet.

Arthur didn't need to guess whether the note was meant for him; someone had already written his name at the top—misspelled Artur—followed by the words *Please Collect*.

The rest of the note was a list. In square capital letters, like a kindergartner's printing, it said:

ARTUR — PLEASE COLLECT

ST. JAMES LIST OF THE
SEVEN MOST IMPORTANT THINGS

1. LIGHTBULBS
2. FOIL
3. MIRRORS
4. PIECES OF WOOD
5. GLASS BOTTLES
6. COFFEE CANS
7. CARDBOARD

That was when Arthur began to realize he hadn't just been sentenced to work for the Junk Man. He'd been sentenced to *be* the Junk Man.

ELEVEN

Arthur stood there for a long time staring at the sign, trying to decide what to do. Snowflakes melted on his head, and his nose ran. Officer Billie had said no excuses, but nobody could expect him to do a crazy job like this, could they?

The list didn't even make sense. Collect cardboard—one of the seven most important things. In what? The world? The *universe*?

Along with *coffee cans*?

And *foil*?

No way. He wasn't doing it.

So he left the cart right where it was and headed back down the alley, kicking the gravel hard in front of him as he walked. *What a joke*, he thought.

But he had only gone a short distance before his pace began to slow.

He thought about having to tell his mother that he'd

screwed up again. That he'd given up on his probation sentence before he'd even started it. That he'd quit and come home. He was sure she'd probably start crying, which would make Barbara cry.

Then there would be Officer Billie to deal with (and who knows what Officer Billie would do if he was her first kid to screw up). And he'd probably have to face the judge again.

And juvie's bad food and bad showers and bad kids . . .

The more he thought about it, the more Arthur knew he couldn't stand to deal with that mess again. Reluctantly, he turned back toward the garage.

The cart and list were still there waiting for him.

Of course.

As Arthur wrapped his fingers around the grimy metal handle of the cart, he tried to tell himself that pushing a rusty grocery cart around the neighborhood wasn't the worst thing that had happened to him in the last few months. Or the worst thing that could happen to someone in life.

He'd already been through that.

He tried to convince himself that maybe this was just a test. Maybe Judge Warner and Officer Billie wanted to find out how he'd react. They probably figured he'd see the stupid list, give up, and go home. *Just what we'd expect from a no-good kid like Arthur Owens,* they'd say.

Arthur started pushing the cart down the gravel alleyway, determined to prove them wrong. Determined to show he could collect a bunch of junk for a crazy old man.

Ten minutes later, he couldn't stand the test any longer.

The rattling din of the cart was worse than the sound of fingernails on a chalkboard. The jangling noise rang in his ears. It set his teeth on edge. It made his head hurt.

Plus, after he'd gone only a block, one of the front wheels stuck.

Wouldn't budge at all.

Arthur had to lift the cart halfway off the sidewalk and shove it forward. But instead of going straight, the empty cart veered wildly to the right and tipped over in someone's snowy yard. Wheels spun crazily in the air.

He yanked it upright. Hauled it back to the sidewalk. The same wheel stuck again. He kicked it. Hard.

Which actually worked.

For a minute, Arthur was kind of proud of himself. Maybe he had some of his dad's mechanical talent after all. He started moving down the street.

The wheel stuck again.

Arthur swore under his breath. He was sure the people who lived in the houses nearby were laughing their heads off as they watched him wrestle the Junk Man's busted cart a few hundred feet down the block. He noticed one guy standing on his front porch, smoking a cigarette. From the smirk on his face, Arthur could tell he was probably the guy's main entertainment for the morning.

Finally, Arthur half pushed, half dragged the cart back to

Groovy Jim's and shoved it into the alley next to the shop. Nobody had said he had to use the useless thing for his sentence. All he needed was some kind of bag to collect the stuff on his list. He'd ask Groovy Jim.

He pushed open the door of the tattoo shop again. Got another blast of antiseptic smells and Hawaiian music. Tried not to look as angry and frustrated as he felt.

"Hey, kiddo." Groovy Jim looked up from where he was sitting behind the counter, feet up, reading a book. "Back again? You found your guy?"

Arthur shook his head and mumbled, "No, he wasn't there."

"Musta just missed him."

"Yeah, I guess."

Arthur glanced around, trying to come up with a good story. "You got any spare bags?" he said finally. "I'm, uh, collecting stuff for a school project."

"Sure." Groovy Jim pulled his feet off the counter. "I've got a couple of burlap ones from the grocer across the street. How many you need?"

"Just one." Then another idea occurred to Arthur. "And what about some cans or, uh, glass jars?" he added, thinking of the Seven Most Important Things. "You have anything like that?"

Groovy Jim nodded. "Sure. I'll see what I can find."

After Groovy Jim disappeared into the back room, Arthur couldn't help feeling a little guilty for lying to a guy who'd been nice and helpful so far. But how could he tell him that he was collecting garbage because he'd thrown a brick at a person's head? And even worse, that it was a person Groovy Jim knew?

Arthur had never been a good liar. Not even about silly things, like pretending to believe in Santa Claus for Barbara at Christmas. And not when it had come to serious things, like covering up for his dad's drinking sometimes.

Christmas.

The sudden thought of what they would do for Christmas without his dad hit Arthur like a fist in the stomach. This was the kind of stuff he still couldn't deal with. He'd been in juvie for Thanksgiving, so he hadn't had to face his first holiday without his dad. But how would they get through Christmas?

And not just this Christmas either. His dad would be gone *every* Christmas. And every birthday. And every holiday from now on. *Forever.*

Thinking about it all, Arthur couldn't breathe.

Fortunately, the clattering crash of a half-dozen ginger ale cans hitting the floor and rolling in all directions snapped him back to reality.

"Jeez oh pete!" Groovy Jim glanced helplessly at the cans he'd dropped on the floor as he came back into the room. "Man, sorry about that!"

After they'd picked up the cans—and Groovy Jim added an empty Skippy jar he'd been using as a pencil holder— Arthur forced himself to focus on the Seven Most Important Things. To not think about his dad. Or the future. All he had to do was find a few more things to keep the Junk Man happy and he'd be done for that Saturday.

Only 116 more hours to go.

"Good luck with your school project," Groovy Jim called out as Arthur left. "You should ask Hampton for some stuff if you see him. He's always collecting things."

"Okay, yeah, I will," Arthur said over his shoulder.

Yet another lie.

TWELVE

Outside, the air felt colder this time around, and the December afternoon had gotten gloomier. The snow looked like white BB pellets coming down from the sky.

Arthur swung the bag of soda pop cans over his shoulder, wincing at the noise, and glanced up and down the street, looking for anything that might fit the Junk Man's list. A lot of people had their garbage cans out, so Saturday had to be a collection day in the neighborhood. Fortunately, the garbage trucks hadn't finished their pickup yet.

In front of the small grocery store across the street, Arthur noticed a stack of flattened cardboard boxes wrapped with twine. Perfect. He crossed the street to pick up an armload of them and brought them back to the cart, since it was a lot easier than hauling a bunch of soggy cardboard around with him all afternoon.

Most Important Thing #7: Cardboard. Done.

Farther down the street, Arthur found a lamp in some-body else's trash pile. He could see why they'd thrown it out—it looked like an ugly turquoise teardrop. Plus, it had a big chip out of one side, and it was missing its bulb and shade.

Still, Arthur figured finding an entire lamp was probably way better than finding a lightbulb. He carried the lamp back to the cart.

Most Important Thing #1: Lightbulbs. Done.

But the toaster was his best discovery.

He'd just reached the end of the block when he spotted the silver toaster sitting on a row of trash cans, as if it was waiting for breakfast.

There was an old lady walking by with a bag of groceries at the same time, so Arthur decided to ask her if she thought the toaster was being thrown out—just to be sure—before he took it.

"You think I can take that thing?" He pointed nervously at the toaster.

The lady gave him a sympathetic look and then squinted at the house behind them. "I don't know the people who live there, but if it's in the garbage, I'm sure you can have it if you need it, young man."

Feeling his face start to get red, Arthur picked up the toaster and hurried back to the cart. He didn't turn around again until he was sure the lady was gone.

Later, he found a dented hubcap by the curb. Another shiny thing. And for Most Important Thing #4, Pieces of Wood, he pulled a couple of evergreen branches from a messy pile of shrubbery trimmings beside somebody's driveway.

By three o'clock, he was finished.

As he hauled the grocery cart out of its spot next to Groovy Jim's shop and dumped the contents of the burlap bag inside, he thought the first Saturday of his probation had gone pretty well.

It was true he hadn't found all of the things on the Junk Man's list. He'd given up on mirrors, for instance. Really— how often did most people throw out a *mirror*?

And he'd switched around a few other things on the list. He'd left ginger ale cans instead of coffee cans. A lamp instead of lightbulbs. And he'd found the really nice toaster and the hubcap instead of foil. But he figured the Junk Man wouldn't mind. He'd gotten close enough, right?

However, Arthur Owens would soon find out . . . the Junk Man did mind.

And close enough wasn't nearly good enough.

THIRTEEN

It was Monday afternoon, two days after Arthur's visit to the Junk Man's garage, when Officer Billie called. Barbara, who wasn't very good at taking messages, had answered the phone.

"A person just called for you," Barbara announced as Arthur walked into the living room. She was curled up on the couch eating a bag of Cheetos and watching cartoons. Usually, Arthur got home before his sister. But it was his first day back at junior high after his time in juvie. The day hadn't gone very well, and then his bus had been late.

"Who was it?" Arthur asked.

"I don't know, but I think she said she was a police officer lady."

Arthur felt his stomach drop. It had to have been Officer Billie.

"Did you do something wrong again?" Barbara pressed

her cheddar-orange lips together like a disapproving gold-fish.

"No."

"Well, she said you need to call her right away."

Arthur went to the kitchen phone and dialed the officer's number reluctantly, hoping she'd gone home for the day. Or the year.

Of course, she answered on the first ring.

"Officer Wanda Billie," a box-shaped voice said.

"This is Arthur Owens."

There was a long silence. Arthur wasn't sure if Officer Billie was trying to remember who he was. Or if he'd already said the wrong thing.

"I spoke with Mr. Hampton today," the chilly voice finally continued. "And he informed me that you did not follow the directions he gave you on Saturday. Is that correct, Mr. Owens?"

"No. I mean—yes, I did follow the directions." Arthur stumbled over his words. "But some things on the list didn't make any sense, so I found a couple of other things for him instead." He tried to explain how he'd left the blue lamp instead of lightbulbs, and how he'd found the hubcap and the toaster instead of foil.

"But everything else he asked for was there. Pretty much . . ." Arthur's voice trailed off as he realized he was making about as much sense as his mom when she got upset. Plus, Officer Billie didn't seem to be listening anyhow.

Or to care.

"I didn't ask you for a list of excuses," she replied flatly. "I asked if you followed Mr. Hampton's specific directions."

"No," Arthur mumbled. "Not exactly all of them."

"Next time, *follow the directions* Mr. Hampton gives you. I don't want to hear from him again. Is that clear?" Officer Billie bellowed into the phone, and then hung up.

Arthur heard himself saying "Yes, ma'am" to the dial tone.

FOURTEEN

Arthur's first week back at school was about as successful as his first day of probation had been. Going from juvie to school was like going from one extreme to the other. In juvie, you learned to avoid everyone else. If some convict kid wanted to cut in front of you in the food line or steal your banana pudding at supper, you let him, no questions asked.

When Arthur got back to school in December, everybody avoided *him*. He felt as if he were inside an invisible box. Nobody bumped into him in the hallway. Nobody spoke to him. When he sat down in the cafeteria for lunch, the other kids picked up their trays and left.

The whole school knew what he'd done, of course. Nothing was a secret at Byrd Junior High. You couldn't fart without somebody knowing.

On Arthur's first day back, the vice principal, who everybody called Vice, although his name was Mr. Barber, met him at the front door after he got off the bus. He always reminded Arthur of a dry cornstalk. Tall guy. Gray wisps of hair on his head. Grim-colored suits.

"Follow me," Vice said, gripping Arthur firmly by one shoulder and steering him down an almost-deserted hallway. "We've moved you."

Arthur wasn't sure what "moved" meant until Vice showed him his new locker in the gym hallway. It was at the opposite end of the school from the other seventh graders' lockers. It didn't take a genius to figure out they'd decided to put him there to keep him away from everybody else.

Plus, the coaches' offices were nearby. Arthur figured the coaches had probably been told to keep a close eye on him and tackle him or something if he did anything violent.

For some reason, the thought of the balding, overweight football coaches trying to tackle him made Arthur smile.

"What's so funny?" Vice asked.

"Nothing," Arthur replied quickly.

"This one is yours." Vice opened metal locker 1034, which smelled like foot odor.

"Okay," Arthur said, glancing inside, although there was nothing to see except a crumpled Oh Henry! candy bar wrapper in the bottom.

Vice closed the locker again with a clang. "So this is where you'll be for a while. Until we see how things are going. With good behavior, you might be able to earn your way back to the seventh-grade hallway someday."

From the doubtful tone of Vice's voice, Arthur guessed

that no matter how good he was, someday was probably never going to come.

Later in the week, Arthur had a big quiz in his earth science class. He'd thought he understood the material pretty well. He knew about volcanoes and earthquakes and how continental drift is the way the continents move. He remembered some of the facts he'd learned before juvie: how we're all living on big plates that are floating around—nothing is permanent—and how some people are unlucky enough to live in places where the plates already have big cracks in them.

Arthur was convinced he was one of those people.

Despite the gloom and doom, he liked earth science. It was one of the few classes he looked forward to. Industrial arts was another one—maybe because the teacher reminded him a little of his dad. And he never gave out any homework.

But Arthur had missed an entire set of volcano questions on the quiz. Without even trying to be funny, he had to admit to himself that he'd completely *blown* it.

The earth science teacher was a short man from India who everybody called Mr. C because his full name had about twenty letters in it. As he handed the quiz back to Arthur, he shook his head sadly and tapped a dark finger on the missed questions.

"You must follow directions next time," he said.

Follow directions. Arthur wondered if the guy knew Officer Billie.

During his first miserable week back at junior high, when he was failing stuff and forgetting stuff and going to his foot-odor locker in the gym hall, Arthur often thought about giving up and quitting. His dad had dropped out of school in the eleventh grade. Can you drop out of school in seventh grade? he wondered. And why bother to learn all this crap anyway? What's the use? What does it matter?

But whenever he thought about quitting, he'd hear Judge Warner saying, *The apple doesn't fall far from the tree.* And it would make him mad enough to stay.

FIFTEEN

Arthur Owens could hardly drag himself out of the house for his second Saturday of probation the next weekend. It was snowing big, wet flakes. The streets were full of slush.

He had no idea what kind of job the Junk Man would dream up for him to do this time. He really hoped he wasn't going to be pushing the rust-bucket cart around the neighborhood collecting junk from a list again. But just in case, he dug out his oldest winter coat to wear.

It was a heavy beige jacket that had these ridiculous pockets and buckles. He'd last worn it in fifth grade, probably. It might have been cool back then, but it definitely wasn't cool anymore. He was amazed—and dismayed—to find that it still fit, except for the sleeves being a couple inches short.

Arthur stuck some folded grocery bags in the pockets, and he made sure to wear a pair of gloves and a hat this time. As he pulled on the black knit hat, he tried not to think about how much he was beginning to act like the Junk Man. Old tan coat. Pockets stuffed with paper bags. All he needed was a pair of foggy eyeglasses, and the transformation would be complete.

"Where did you find that thing?" his mother said, catching him in the hallway before he left.

Arthur shrugged. "Back of the closet."

She gave him a curious look. "Did you lose your other coat?"

"No." Arthur avoided her gaze.

He could tell his mom wanted to ask more questions, but she didn't. He hadn't told her about the deserted garage or about collecting the Seven Most Important Things yet. And he'd managed to make sure Barbara didn't blab about Officer Billie's phone call. Why make his mom worry even more?

Before Arthur's first day of probation, his mom had called Officer Billie to make sure working for the Junk Man was safe. "When we see him around our neighborhood, sometimes the man acts a little strange," she'd explained.

Officer Billie had told Arthur's mom that she should be way more worried about her brick-throwing son than Mr. Hampton—a comment that really irritated her. "That lady doesn't know you like I do," she'd said in a huff as she hung up the phone.

Knowing what his mom was like, all Arthur had told her was that he'd been running errands for Mr. Hampton. "It was pretty easy," he'd said after his first Saturday. "He gave me a list of things to get for him."

It wasn't a complete lie, even if his mom thought he meant he'd gone shopping.

As Arthur got ready to leave for his second Saturday of work, his mom patted his back and tried to sound encouraging. "Be as helpful as you were last week for Mr. Hampton and maybe he'll let you off early."

Arthur knew there was no chance of that happening. Not with Officer Billie keeping track of every second.

"We'll work on the Christmas tree when you get back, all right?" his mom continued. "Before Barbara gets home from her friend's house."

"Sure. Okay. See you later," Arthur said, quickly yanking the door shut behind him. He didn't want his mom to see his face and realize how much he was dreading the Christmas tree. Actually, he was dreading it way more than his four hours of work for the Junk Man.

Arthur's father had always been the one who put up the tree.

Two weeks before Christmas, he'd drag the boxes down from the attic to assemble the fake tree and do the lights. It took him hours and never put him in a good mood. But when it was finished, it was a work of art. That was what he used to call it, "a work of art." Some years, they'd leave his "work of art" up until February, when Arthur's mother would have to dust off the branches before they put it away.

This year, the tree was still in the attic. Arthur knew his mother and Barbara were counting on him to take his dad's place, but he couldn't bear to think about putting up the tree himself. Not yet.

As he slogged through the slushy streets to the Junk Man's neighborhood, he tried to get his mind to focus on something else. What kinds of crazy stuff would the Junk Man have him searching for this Saturday? he wondered. Toilet paper rolls? Cigarette butts? Used toothbrushes?

He didn't think he'd ever be able to find a mirror, if that was still on the list. Or lightbulbs. Heck, he'd just borrow one from a lamp at home if he had to. He wasn't going to waste his time scrounging around for a stupid lightbulb.

What he'd like to find was a good pair of boots. He glanced down at the pair he was wearing. The rubber soles were cracked and already leaking. A slow dampness crept up from his toes.

Since the weather outside was so crummy, he thought maybe Mr. Hampton would have him working on something inside the garage instead. Then he decided it would be better if that didn't happen. He had no idea what he'd say if he finally met the guy face to face. Or what the guy might say to him.

Fortunately, the garage was deserted when Arthur got there. As he walked up the gravel alleyway, he could see that the door with the drippy address numbers was firmly closed. The side door was locked. And the cart sat in the same spot he'd left it the week before.

From a distance, the cart appeared to have everything he'd collected still piled inside it too: The ugly turquoise lamp. The toaster. The ginger ale cans. The dented hubcap. The tree branches.

Clearly, Officer Billie was right. The Junk Man hadn't liked any of it.

As Arthur got closer, he realized a few things were different, though. Some of the cardboard was gone. And the silver temperature knob had mysteriously disappeared from the toaster. (At least, Arthur thought it had been attached when he'd left the toaster there.)

Arthur also noticed a different sign taped to the grocery cart handle. He stepped nearer to read what it said.

The first part of the message was the same list of Seven Most Important Things he'd been given the week before, with the same misspelled *Artur* at the top.

But at the bottom of the sign, the Junk Man had added a few more words. In blue ballpoint pen, he'd written a quote:

"WHERE THERE IS NO VISION, THE PEOPLE PERISH."

Arthur had no idea what it meant, but he was pretty sure it wasn't supposed to be a compliment.

SIXTEEN

Arthur decided to ask Groovy Jim if he'd ever heard the saying before. Just in case there was some hidden point he was supposed to get.

Arthur was never good at finding the hidden points in things—especially not if it was in his English class. He'd missed most of *Romeo and Juliet* while he was in juvie, but he got back in time to find out that almost everyone in the play dies at the end. This was the only hidden point he'd gotten from *Romeo and Juliet:*

Everybody dies.

Groovy Jim didn't seem to mind the interruption.

"Hey, kiddo, you're back," he said when Arthur pushed open the door of the shop. "Come on in." He waved a tattooed arm. "I could use some company here. I'm turning into a block of boredom."

Arthur glanced around the empty shop, which smelled faintly of peppermint this time. It looked like Groovy Jim had added a couple new posters of tattoo designs on the walls. One of comic-book characters. Another of sailing ships. There was a string of droopy tinsel across the front of the counter where he was sitting. Arthur had no idea how the guy stayed in business. He never seemed to have any customers, although Arthur guessed that getting a tattoo in the middle of winter probably wasn't very popular.

As Arthur closed the door behind him, he realized he hadn't planned out exactly what his story would be. What would he give as a reason for being there two Saturdays in a row? And how would he explain why Mr. Hampton was leaving him bizarre quotes on pieces of cardboard?

"So, what can I do for you?" Groovy Jim asked as Arthur stood awkwardly just inside the door. "You looking for Mr. Hampton again?"

"Yeah, kind of." Arthur reached into his pocket for the scrap of cardboard, still debating what to ask. "He left me this note and I have no clue what it means." Slowly, he read the words to Groovy Jim. "Have you ever heard that saying before?"

Groovy Jim laughed. "Sure, I've got the same one right here." He tapped his finger on a piece of paper taped to his counter. "Hampton likes to hand it out a lot. Grocery guy across the street has the same quote taped on his counter too."

Arthur stepped closer to see. It was written on an old, creased note card. Same blue pen as on his cardboard note. Same square printed letters.

"What does it mean?"

Groovy Jim shrugged. "Beats me. Hampton, he's deep, man."

"Deep?"

"Smart. Philosophical. Way beyond ordinary folks like you and me." Groovy Jim leaned back in his chair and rested his feet on top of the counter. He was wearing bedroom slippers, Arthur noticed. In the middle of the day.

"See, most people don't get the guy at all," Groovy Jim continued. "All they see is some far-out dude going around town with a cart full of junk. They think he's nuts. But I'm telling you, Hampton is way deeper than people realize. Trust me, he's got a good reason for everything he says and does."

"What reason?"

"Well, that's a question you'll have to ask him yourself. Can't help you with that one, kiddo."

Arthur couldn't tell if Groovy Jim was avoiding the question or if he really didn't know anything more about Mr. Hampton.

Groovy Jim tapped his finger on the note card. "Now, if you want my opinion of what the quote means, I think it is trying to say if you don't have vision—if you don't look deeper and see the possibilities in things—your spirit, your soul, will die." He squinted at Arthur. "Get it?"

No, Arthur didn't really get it—and he especially didn't get what his spirit had to do with collecting garbage. How was he supposed to look deeper at a coffee can, for instance?

But he pretended he understood. "Yeah, I see what you mean. Thanks."

"Well, I hope you find what you're looking for this morning." Groovy Jim nodded and picked up a magazine from the counter. "Stay warm."

It was only later, after Arthur left, that he realized he hadn't actually told Groovy Jim he was looking for anything that morning.

SEVENTEEN

After all the talk about vision and looking deeper for things, it was ironic that the first thing Arthur spotted after he left Groovy Jim's was a mirror.

It was leaning against some garbage cans at a house a few doors down the street. Arthur was trying to get the grocery cart to move through the slush—he'd cleared out the stuff from the week before and decided to bring the cart along just in case he needed it—when he saw the corner of something catch the reflection of a passing car. He sprinted toward the trash pile as if it might suddenly vanish.

Yes, it really was a mirror.

As Arthur tugged it out of the wet, snow-covered pile, he couldn't believe his good luck. One corner had a long, diagonal crack, and there were a few specks of tarnish on the surface, but the rest was perfect. A slam dunk. He felt like pumping his fist in the air or doing some kind of victory dance. He had scored a mirror in the first five minutes—no, the first five seconds—of his search.

Then he realized how totally nuts it was to be celebrating a *broken mirror.* What in the world was he thinking?

Quickly, he jammed his hands in his coat pockets and pretended to be interested in something down the street. A cop had stopped to help a VW Beetle with a flat. Arthur waited until the cop had his back turned and some other cars had passed by before he grabbed the mirror, stuck it under his right arm, and hurried to the cart.

On the next street, things got even better.

Arthur found a nice polished table—the kind you'd put at the end of a sofa—sitting by someone's curb. It had curved legs and some gold leafy designs painted on the top. The only thing it was missing was a drawer in the front.

Since the Junk Man hadn't liked the straggly branches he'd left the week before, Arthur thought maybe he hadn't really wanted "pieces of wood" like branches. He'd meant pieces *made* of wood. Like furniture. Which made more sense when Arthur thought about all the broken furniture the Junk Man used to haul around the neighborhood in his cart.

In which case, the table would be perfect.

Carefully, Arthur lifted the square table and set it sideways in the cart. It was too big to carry, so he was glad he'd brought the cart. He only hoped its stubborn wheels would keep working.

Pulling the black knit cap down farther over his head, he tried not to notice all of the cars slowing to check out what he was doing. He was sure it probably looked as if he was stealing stuff from half the neighborhood as he started down the street again with the big mirror and table legs sticking out of his cart.

The wet snow was falling harder, which he was glad about. Maybe people would pay more attention to the snow than him.

Foil. Coffee cans. Lightbulbs. Those turned out to be a lot more difficult. Arthur began to realize he could keep his eyes open all day and probably never spot any of them lying around outside, waiting to be picked up as a Most Important Thing.

It would be easier to find a discarded toilet—he had seen several of those already.

Eventually, Arthur knew he had no choice. If he wanted to find everything on the list, he would have to look *inside* a few garbage cans.

The first garbage can was the worst.

Arthur chose a house where nobody seemed to be home. It was a block away from Mr. Hampton's garage. There was a green tinsel wreath on the door, but all the windows were dark. There were no cars in the driveway.

Arthur waited until there were no cars coming down the street either. He tried to look like he was just passing by the empty house. With an old grocery cart. Checking out the neighborhood garbage cans. For fun.

The trash can he chose to open appeared to be pretty new—which Arthur thought was a good thing—but the metal lid was slick from the wet snow. The suction created by the water and metal meant he had to work to get the lid free.

Using just one hand to pull wasn't enough. Gloves didn't help—they slipped too much. He had to use his bare hands. He grabbed the handle and tugged. Hard.

With one sudden pop, the lid came off. Water splattered across the front of Arthur's coat. A lot of curse words splattered out of his mouth.

As he stood there with who-knows-what all over him, Arthur tried to tell himself there were worse things in life. Being covered in trash water wasn't as bad as having a rusty razor held to your neck, right?

Sure.

Arthur exhaled slowly. He said a few more swearwords to make himself feel better. Then he forced himself to take one step forward and peer into the disgusting depths of the garbage can. He would find something useful inside it, no matter what.

And right there on top, like they were waiting for him, were some foil TV dinner trays. Not too clean, but the list didn't say *clean* foil, did it?

He pulled them out one by one. Three Hungry Chef TV dinner trays. The sight of them put a familiar lump in

Arthur's throat. He used to eat Hungry Chef dinners with his dad in front of the television whenever his mother worked late at the waitressing job she had.

Turkey and mashed potatoes with extra stuffing had been their favorite. Usually, they'd eat one each and split a third.

"Hungry Chef and a half," his dad used to joke.

Arthur had tried them again, not too long ago. He'd cooked two when his mom was working late and he was watching Barbara. But he couldn't finish more than a few bites.

"You want to have this one?" he'd asked Barbara, holding out the second steamy tray, which he hadn't even touched.

"No," she'd said, turning up her nose. "I don't." For some reason, it really bugged him. He'd told Barbara that she was a spoiled little brat, and the whole night kind of went downhill from there.

Arthur tossed the trays into his cart and slammed the lid back on the trash can. He needed to stop remembering things and do his work. Checking his watch, he sighed. He still had three hours to go.

The last things he collected that Saturday were the lightbulbs. He'd just found two coffee cans and decided it was time to give up. He hoped the nice wooden table and the big mirror and all the foil trays—people had eaten a lot of TV dinners that week—would make up for not finding Most Important Thing #1: Lightbulbs.

But then, as he was heading back to the garage, he noticed a tangled knot of discarded Christmas lights next to someone's trash can. A few of the bulbs were missing, but the string still had more than enough left. The Junk Man could even choose from two different colors: white or green. Arthur tossed the Christmas lights on top of his pile.

Done.

As he pushed and pulled the stubborn cart back to Mr. Hampton's garage, he decided nobody could accuse him of not following directions this Saturday. Of not having "vision." He'd found everything on the list, including a pretty decent table.

What he really wanted to know was why. That's what kept circling through his mind. Groovy Jim had said the guy always had a reason for what he did. So what was it? Why did Mr. Hampton want coffee cans but not ginger ale cans? Or lightbulbs but not lamps?

The list seemed totally random and pointless, but Arthur was beginning to think maybe it wasn't.

THE FIRST IMPORTANT THING

"How did it go?" Arthur's mom asked cheerfully when he got home, as if he'd been out doing something fun, instead of serving four hours of his probation sentence. "Was Mr. Hampton nice to you?"

"Sure." Arthur shoved his coat into the back of the closet, hoping his mom didn't notice anything different about it. Hoping it didn't smell.

"What did you do today?"

"Just moved some furniture and helped find some Christmas tree lights. Nothing big," he said, keeping his eyes down as he tugged off his boots.

Too late, he realized the mistake he'd made.

His mom smiled and wiped her hands on her apron. "Good. Let's get *our* Christmas tree down from the attic now that you're back."

So Arthur had no choice, really. He couldn't exactly tell

his mom he was still hoping his dad's accident had been a bad dream and maybe, if they waited, he would be there to put up the tree for them. That would sound crazy and sad, and it would probably make her cry.

"Sure," he said, keeping his voice as normal as he could. "No problem, Mom. I can do it."

"I'll help you pull down the steps."

After the two of them had unfolded the narrow ladder that led to the attic, Arthur climbed up, while his mom stood at the bottom with a pencil-sized flashlight giving completely unhelpful advice.

"Be careful," she kept saying. "Your dad would always hit his head going up. And watch out for nails in the floor. You don't want to get a rusty nail in your hand. There should be a light once you get up there. Look for the chain. There should be a chain to pull. But watch out for your head. You don't want to hit your head."

"I got it, Mom!" he yelled, probably louder than he needed to.

A lump rose in Arthur's throat as he pulled on the light and saw all the stuff from their past piled in the attic: The cans of paint his dad had used when Arthur's mom wanted the kitchen painted a bright banana yellow. Racks of clothes. Boxes of Arthur's old Matchbox cars and racetracks.

Arthur remembered how his dad used to spend hours with him when he was a little kid, playing with those cars. Putting the black plastic tracks all over the living room. Figure eights around the coffee table. Ramps on the sofa cushions.

Did that kind of thing count at all in heaven? Would God care that his dad had been perfect at playing Matchbox cars, even if he'd had a lot of other faults?

And then Arthur got mad at himself for wondering about such stupid things.

"Are you doing okay up there?" His mother's worried voice drifted up from below. The little dot from her flashlight flitted on the ceiling above him like an irritating bug. "Can you see the tree box and the lights?"

Arthur dragged his attention back to looking for the tree. He finally spotted the box in the far corner of the attic. It said ULTRA-REAL ARTIFICIAL TREE and had a cartoon of a dancing elf on it.

Arthur resisted the urge to kick the box.

Instead, he hollered, "Got it, Mom!" and began pushing the big box toward the steps. He had no clue how he would get it down the narrow stairs. Probably his dad had carried it on his shoulder like a real man.

Arthur knew there was no way he could do the same thing. His shoulder muscles were about as real as the ultra-real Christmas tree.

He decided to try sliding it down the stairs. He told his mom to stay out of the way. One step at a time—with his arms grasping the slick sides of the box—Arthur made his way backward down the narrow, creaky steps.

"Careful, honey," his mom kept repeating, as if this would keep him safe. "What you're doing looks very dangerous."

Of course this is dangerous! Arthur wanted to yell at his mother. *That's why Dad should be here doing it and not me.*

His father had always loved doing dangerous things (usually stuff he didn't tell Arthur's mom about until later). Drag racing with his buddies when he was younger. Carving the curves with his motorcycle. Doing spinouts in parking lots. Staying out late and drinking too much sometimes. Arthur's mom often said Tom Owens's biggest problem was that he never grew up.

Once they got the box safely into the living room, Arthur's mom offered to help put the tree together, but he didn't think he could stand having her around, fussing about every little thing. Plus, he just wanted to be sad and angry at his dad by himself.

"That's okay," he told her impatiently. "I can do it."

"You sure you don't need any help?" His mom looked like she was getting upset.

Arthur sighed. "All right, okay."

"Wait." She stuck her finger in the air. "I'll go and make us some hot chocolate before we start."

Neither one of them mentioned how Arthur's dad had often put up the tree while polishing off a six-pack of beer.

While his mother was in the kitchen, Arthur started pulling the fake branches out of the box. The pile looked like a mangled tree puzzle when he was finished. Strands of old tinsel stuck to his shirt.

When she returned with the mugs of hot chocolate, his mom burst out laughing. "Maybe we should decorate you instead."

Not really amused, Arthur brushed himself off. "Where do you want to start?"

"I'm not sure." His mom stared at the project in front of them, looking lost.

They decided to begin at the bottom. Arthur's mom untangled the musty, attic-smelling branches while Arthur kneeled on the floor and stuck them in the tiny holes of the fake-tree stand.

After he'd put about eight branches on one side, the whole tree fell over. An explosion of needles and branches landed on Arthur's back.

He swore under his breath. His mom laughed. In fact, she collapsed on the sofa, laughing so hard Arthur worried that maybe she was going nuts. He couldn't remember the last time he'd heard his mother laugh like that.

She sounded like a crazed hyena.

"Stop it, Mom, or I'm quitting," Arthur said, feeling more teed off the longer she went on. The damn tree had fallen on him. His dad was dead. And his mom was completely losing it.

"Oh, I'm not laughing at you, hon. I'm just laughing at . . ." His mom sat on the edge of the sofa and tried to catch her breath. "I don't know . . . I guess at how everything in our life keeps falling apart, no matter what we do. Then, to top it off, even our sad old Christmas tree goes and falls over on us."

"Not funny," Arthur said in an irritated voice. "And it fell on me, not you."

"Knocked out by a Christmas tree," his mom said, with just a hint of a smile.

"Stop it."

"KO'd by Christmas. Ho, ho, ho," she added.

And then she dissolved into laughter again, and Arthur found himself unable to keep from laughing too. He didn't even know why. There was a huge lump in his throat, and he wanted to cry or hit something—and yet here he was, laughing with his mom.

It was official. They really had lost their minds.

"Okay, we have to get the tree up before your sister comes back from her friend's house," his mom announced, trying to regain her composure. She pushed up the sleeves of her blouse and took charge. "You hold the tree, Artie. And I'll stick the branches in."

With the two of them working, the tree project went faster. It wasn't until they were halfway finished that Arthur and his mom realized the branches were different sizes— smaller ones for the top and larger ones for the bottom.

"Well, how were we supposed to know that?" Arthur's mom looked annoyed as she stared at the half-built tree, hands on her hips.

Once he stepped back, Arthur could see that their Christmas tree did have a funny shape. More like a green hedge than a tree.

"Well, who cares," his mom snapped. "We are just going to stick these branches wherever we damn well please."

Arthur wisely kept quiet while his mom finished jamming the branches into the trunk, mumbling to herself.

The lights and decorations were the final steps.

Arthur's dad had always been a perfectionist about the lights. Maybe it came from being a mechanic, but he'd been fanatical about making sure every wire was hidden, every bulb tucked into the branches. There couldn't be any dark spots. Black holes, his father had called them.

Arthur and his mom were not perfectionists. They strung the lights around the tree in less than five minutes. There were a lot of dark spots and black holes.

But none of that seemed to matter to Barbara.

She got home as Arthur and his mother were cleaning up. They had just finished putting the extra tree branches into the box and were picking up all the scraps from the carpet when Barbara came barreling through the front door with the usual armload of dolls she carried to her friends' houses.

"It's our Christmas tree!" Her eyes widened in surprise at the sight of the sparkling tree—well, hedge—in the living room.

"Your brother put it up," their mom said proudly. "We still have to decorate it."

"Thank you, Arthur!" Dropping her dolls in the middle of the hallway, Barbara raced across the living room. Her blond head dove into Arthur's stomach. He didn't want to look like a wimp, but she had a pretty hard head for a seven-year-old. He tried not to wince.

"It looks like magic with all the lights," his sister said,

clasping her hands and stepping back to stare at the tree again, as if she had never seen one before. "Let's turn everything off so we can see it better."

Arthur's mom switched off the living room lamps.

As they stood there in the darkness, with little sunbursts of light from the tree shining on their clothes and faces, Arthur felt strangely hopeful for a minute. It was as if their old life had briefly flickered back on, like an old movie—as if none of the bad things had happened to them yet.

Barbara, who could be a real pain in the butt sometimes, had this sweet, angelic expression on her face. His mom was smiling and not crying. And the tree didn't look half as bad as he'd thought it would.

It had to be the lights, he decided. That's what made the difference.

Without realizing it, Arthur had discovered the first important thing.

EIGHTEEN

Arthur got two weeks off from his probation for Christmas. Of course, he still had 112 more hours to serve, so it wasn't really a gift or anything. Officer Billie gave him the news. He wasn't expecting her visit.

In fact, when Arthur looked out the window and saw a cop car pulling into their driveway late on Monday afternoon, his first panicked thought was that something bad had happened to his mom and Barbara.

They'd gone shopping after school because Barbara needed new shoes and his mom needed a nice dress to wear for a big job interview she had at a dentist's office on Wednesday. The dentist was looking for a full-time receptionist. If his mom got the job, it would mean she could quit her two lousy part-time waitressing ones. Arthur was trying not to hope too much, but he really wanted her to get it.

When Officer Billie stepped out of the car, Arthur released the shaky breath he'd been holding. At least he knew everything was okay with his mom and Barbara—even if it probably wasn't okay for him.

The officer was carrying something as she came up to the front door. From a distance, Arthur couldn't tell what it was, but it looked like some type of round container. He figured it was from the Junk Man. Returning something else he didn't like.

As he fumbled to open the door for Officer Billie, Arthur wished he weren't wearing the wrinkled jeans and under-shirt he'd thrown on when he got home from school. He also hoped he didn't have peanut butter on his teeth from the sandwich he'd been eating.

"May I come in for a minute, Mr. Owens?" Officer Billie said in her official cop voice when he finally got the door open.

"Sure, okay, yes," Arthur said in a rush, stumbling backward to let her in.

As the officer stepped inside and took off her cap, Arthur glanced around nervously, worrying what she might notice. The collection of dirty glasses on the coffee table? Barbara's paper dolls strewn all over the living room? The misshapen Christmas tree? The stacks of unopened and unpaid bills drifting out of the bookshelves?

"I have come on official and unofficial business," Officer Billie stated, remaining squarely in the middle of the hall-way. "First, the official part: I have not received any further complaints from Mr. Hampton, so I assume you followed his directions successfully on Saturday. Is that right, Mr. Owens?"

"Yes, ma'am. I guess so," Arthur replied carefully, wondering if the officer had any clue what the directions were.

"Well, I expect this will continue to be the case," Officer Billie said crisply. "However," she continued, "Mr. Hampton has informed me that he will be away for the Christmas holiday, so he has requested that you be given two weeks off from your probation. Your work for him will resume on the first Saturday in January. Is that clear?"

Arthur nodded.

"Here. I've written down the date for you. Saturday, January fourth." Officer Billie handed him a piece of paper. "And now for the unofficial business." She held out a cookie tin with a rocking horse on the top. "Every Christmas, I make caramel corn for my kids. It's my specialty," she explained. "Merry Christmas."

Arthur had no idea how to reply. Officer Billie wasn't the kind of person you'd expect to get a gift from. Especially not something she'd made. It also took him a minute to realize that when the officer said "my kids," she probably wasn't talking about her real kids—she meant juvenile delinquents like him.

"*Stop.*" Officer Billie's hand went up as the awkward silence continued. "When someone gives you a gift, it is polite to look them in the eye and say in a clear and appreciative voice, 'Thank you very much.'"

Arthur forced his eyes upward. "Thank you very much."

"You're welcome," Officer Billie replied. She pointed one of her square fingers at him. "Share it with your family. And don't mess up over the next couple of weeks. A lot of people mess up over Christmas. It's a tough season. Don't let me catch you being one of them."

Arthur nodded. "Okay."

Officer Billie put on her cap. "Have a good evening." She pulled the door closed behind her with a firm, official-sounding thud.

After she left, Arthur leaned against the door, still holding the caramel corn and feeling kind of shaken up. People could surprise you, he thought.

NINETEEN

Officer Billie was right about one thing, Arthur discovered. Despite having the least sweet personality of anybody he knew, she made awfully good caramel corn.

And she was also right about another thing.

Christmas was a very tough season.

The one bright spot was that his mom got the receptionist job. The dentist called a few days before Christmas and told her she could start in January. After his mom got off the phone with her new boss, she sat down on the kitchen floor and started crying into a dish towel because she was so happy. That's what she told Arthur when he came running into the kitchen to check if she was okay—she was crying because she was happy.

Sometimes he gave up trying to figure out his mom.

•••

Christmas Day was a different story. If it had been up to Arthur, he would have pulled the covers over his head and pretended it was a regular day. But Barbara and his mom were counting on him.

So when Barbara poked him in the arm at about six o'clock and whispered loudly in his ear that Santa had been there, he managed to say "Good, let's see" in a fake excited voice. He followed his sister's polka-dot robe downstairs.

"Merry Christmas, guys!" Arthur's mom said extra cheerfully as they came into the living room. She'd put on bright pink lipstick, even though it was six in the morning and nobody else was around. "White Christmas" was playing on the record player. The air smelled faintly of burned cinnamon rolls.

Arthur could tell his mom was trying hard to make Christmas nice for them. But it seemed strange. Like they were actors in a play. Or aliens on a planet that looked exactly like their own, only it wasn't.

Barbara squealed as she tore open her gifts of baby dolls, and paper dolls, and Barbie dolls—and more dolls than Arthur could be bothered to pay attention to. He'd already been warned about the gifts. How there wouldn't be many and most of them would be for Barbara. Money was still tight.

He handed his mother the small gift he'd wrapped for her. "Here, Mom."

"For me?" she said, looking surprised.

"It's nothing, Mom, really."

His mom opened the tissue paper slowly. Inside, there was a small metal flowerpot in the shape of a watering can.

"It's a flowerpot," he explained, just in case she didn't get it.

"I know what it is," she said, still acting surprised. "But you shouldn't have spent money to buy me anything this year. Not with all that's happened. I was fine with nothing."

Arthur shrugged. "That's okay. It wasn't much."

Because the truth was—it was free.

He'd found it on the same Saturday that he'd found the mirror. It had been stuck in a trash can with a bunch of broken clay pots and garden stuff. The silver spout was what he spotted first.

Once he'd managed to pull out the rest of it, Arthur knew it would make the perfect gift for his mom. She always kept a row of African violets on the kitchen windowsill.

He was pretty proud of how it had turned out too. He'd glued the shaky handle back into place and polished the metal with some of his dad's chrome polish. It looked brand-new. If the person who had thrown out the flowerpot could see how nice it looked now, Arthur was sure they would have kept it.

"Well, thank you," his mom said, squeezing his shoulders with one arm. "However much it was. I love it."

As it turned out, Arthur's mom surprised him with a gift too. She handed him a flat box wrapped in green paper. When he opened it, he found his dad's silver-dollar collection. Six mint-condition peace dollars displayed in a black frame.

"I saved these for you. I know your dad wanted you to have them," his mom said softly.

A thick lump rose in Arthur's throat as he remembered looking at these silver coins with his dad. He'd taken them to elementary school a bunch of times for show-and-tell. He'd written a research report about them in third grade called "All About Money." His dad had often said, "One day, when I'm gone, I'll pass them on to you."

Now that he had them, Arthur didn't really want them.

Not now—or ever.

"And I got something for you too, Arthur. Open it! Open it!" Barbara flopped on the sofa next to him. For once, he was grateful to his sister for interrupting something.

She shoved a roundish package covered with way more tape than paper into his hands.

"It's a baseball! Did you guess? Did you guess?" she shouted before he had the wrapping half off.

"Thanks, Barbara. That's really nice," Arthur said, his voice cracking only a little. He tossed the baseball in the air and caught it. "It's perfect."

"I bought it with my own allowance money," she said proudly as Arthur's mom winked at him. "I've been saving all year."

Later, when his mom and Barbara were busy doing dishes in the kitchen, Arthur went upstairs and put the baseball on top of the dresser. He shoved the coins in the back of his closet, though.

It was weird how much they bothered him. He wasn't sure why. When his father's motorcycle cap and coat had been in the downstairs closet, they hadn't bothered him at all. In a way, they had made him feel as if his dad was still there.

But the coins made his throat clench up the minute he looked at them.

Arthur knew his mom was just trying to make up for what had happened in November. He knew she still blamed herself for some of it, even though he'd tried to tell her it wasn't her fault—she wasn't the one who'd lost her cool and hit someone with a brick.

It made Arthur realize how you couldn't always know what things would be important to people and what wouldn't. His mom had thrown out his dad's motorcycle cap, thinking it didn't matter, but it was way more important to Arthur than the silver coins she'd saved. And the flowerpot had been worthless to someone in Mr. Hampton's neighborhood, but it had turned out to be the perfect Christmas gift for his mom.

In other words, there could be a lot of reasons why people decided to save some things and why they threw others away—reasons that might not make any sense until you dug much deeper.

Which, Arthur thought, might be a small clue to the Junk Man's list.

TWENTY

Just to get out of the house, Arthur took a walk to Mr. Hampton's garage on the Saturday after Christmas. It was one of those deceptively sunny but frigid end-of-December days. Arthur's breath made clouds. The snow-covered sidewalks crunched like icebergs under his feet.

He passed by an older guy who was walking a dog wearing a ridiculous sweater. Arthur normally didn't wave to people, but since it was just after Christmas and they were the only ones around, it seemed like the right thing to do.

"My wife knitted it," the guy said, waving back.

Arthur smiled politely and kept going. He wasn't sure what he hoped to find at the garage when he got there, or why he felt the need to go there at all during his two weeks off. It wasn't as if Officer Billie would deduct an hour from his probation for *visiting* the garage. But his curiosity about what Mr. Hampton was doing had gotten the better of him.

Officer Billie had said the guy was going away for the Christmas holidays, but Arthur didn't believe it. A trash picker didn't seem like the kind of person who would take vacations or have a regular family somewhere. It seemed more likely he wanted to work at the garage without being bothered.

Arthur figured if he stopped by unexpectedly, he might get a glimpse of what the guy was up to. The purpose of the Seven Most Important Things still bugged him. He wanted to see what else he could find out.

Of course, the walk turned out to be a complete waste of time.

The garage was locked up and looked as deserted as always. The grocery cart sat in its usual place outside the garage door, with its wheels buried in clumps of snow and ice. Maybe Officer Billie had been right. It didn't seem like anybody had been around the place in days.

Groovy Jim's shop was dark and closed up too. There was a folding iron gate across the doorway, which made the place look a lot more unfriendly than it usually did. A handwritten sign behind the gate said: BACK NEXT YEAR.

It took Arthur a minute to figure out the sign meant he'd be back in a few days, when the new year arrived. Not in 365 days.

Since there was nobody around and nothing to see, he shoved his hands in his pockets and walked home, feeling like an idiot. A cold idiot.

When Arthur returned home, he found Barbara sitting in the middle of the living room floor, munching on a sugar cookie. She was wearing her pink plaid coat and mittens. Crumbs were everywhere.

"What are you doing?" he said. "Where's Mom?"

"She went next door to borrow something. I was playing outside. Then I got hungry, so I came in." Barbara chewed on her crumbly cookie. "Oh, and I talked to your friend too."

Arthur stopped pulling off his boots. He stood in the hallway with one boot on and one off. "What friend?" he said, because he didn't have any friends. Not since his dad's accident and being in juvie. Even before that, he hadn't had a lot of friends. He wasn't the kind of person who liked to hang out in big groups.

His best friend, Ben Branson, who'd lived a few doors down the street, had moved away at the end of fifth grade. They used to play kickball together and trade baseball cards. He still had a couple of his Roger Maris cards.

"Was Ben back here?" he said, glancing out the window. Despite being good friends, they'd never bothered to write much after he left.

"No. Your friend with the shopping cart. You know," Barbara said impatiently, glaring at her brother as if he were a dope, "the old man you threw the thing at but now you're friends with again. That's who."

Arthur stared at his sister. What in the world was she talking about?

"The Junk Man—Mr. Hampton—was here?" he said slowly.

Barbara nodded and took another bite of her cookie. "Well, he didn't have that old cart with him, but I knew it was him when I saw him across the street, so I waved and said 'Hi, mister.' And he came over and shook my hand and told me 'Merry Christmas.'" Barbara stuck out her hand to demonstrate. "So I said 'Merry Christmas' too, and I told him how you were my brother and how you weren't bad anymore now." She smiled proudly. "And I said how you had promised not to throw anything else again. Wasn't that nice of me?" she added.

Arthur couldn't believe what he was hearing. It seemed like way too bizarre a coincidence that he'd been trying to find out more about the Junk Man and maybe, at the same time, the Junk Man had been trying to find out more about him.

"Oh, and I also asked him if his kids got lots of stuff from Santa for Christmas. And he said he doesn't have any kids. Isn't that sad?" Barbara gave an exaggerated frown. "But he said it was okay. He likes being by himself."

Arthur shook his head. How could his little sister have found out more about the Junk Man in five minutes of blabbering than he had?

"What else did he tell you?" Arthur pulled off his other boot. He pretended not to seem too interested in the conversation so his sister wouldn't clam up.

"Well, he told me he doesn't live in our neighborhood. He

lives in three little rooms in a building farther away. And I asked him why he always pushes a shopping cart around, and he said it isn't a shopping cart, it's a chariot, but you just can't see the horses. Isn't that funny?" Barbara laughed. "A chariot—but you just can't see the horses!

"And the best part of all"—she stood up and reached into her coat pocket—"he gave me a pretty silver bead to keep."

She held out her hand.

And there, in his sister's pink mitten, was the missing silver temperature knob from the toaster.

TWENTY-ONE

Arthur had no idea what the silver toaster knob was supposed to mean or why Mr. Hampton had given it to his little sister. He thought he might get some answers when he went back for his first Saturday of probation in January, but nothing had changed. He arrived at Mr. Hampton's garage on January 4 and found the same list and the same cart. Nobody around. No other notes.

Arthur figured maybe it had just been a coincidence—maybe the guy happened to be taking a stroll past their house and had the toaster knob in his pocket, so he decided to give it to Barbara.

But then something happened at school that made Arthur begin to wonder even more about the connections between his work for Mr. Hampton and his life.

• • •

It all started when Arthur forgot his earth science textbook in his locker. It was a couple of days after they got back to school from the Christmas holiday. They were having an open-book quiz. He needed the book.

Normally, he tried to avoid going to his locker to get anything during lunch, when the ninth-grade varsity football players liked to hang around in the gym hallway and goof off. A lot of them were the size of Slash from juvie. Or bigger. Arthur knew it would only be a matter of time before they'd try to test the brick-throwing "juvie kid" for fun. Just to see how tough he really was.

He didn't want them to find out he wasn't very tough at all.

But he knew it would be an instant detention if he didn't have the textbook. And he didn't like disappointing Mr. C. So he ate his lunch quickly, tossed his trash in the garbage, and headed to his locker, hoping to get there before the jocks.

His locker was halfway down the gym hall, just past the water fountains. As he came around the corner, he noticed a big group of guys gathered at the end of the hall. They were huddled around something.

"Crap," he said under his breath.

He considered turning around and going back to the cafeteria. He'd just blow off the quiz, he told himself. Who cared?

But the group had already spotted him. If he didn't want to look like a total wimp, he had to keep walking toward his locker.

He tried to seem preoccupied with what was outside the hallway windows—as if he wasn't paying attention to the jocks and didn't care what bad stuff they were doing. He'd just go to his locker, get his book, and leave. They could do whatever they wanted. It wasn't his problem.

It was the laughter that forced Arthur to take another look. He'd heard that kind of raucous laughter before. In juvie, it always meant trouble.

In the middle of the jocks' huddle at the end of the hallway, he noticed one of the big gray trash cans from the cafeteria. As he watched, one guy reached behind his back for a basketball and suddenly whipped the ball at the side of the can. It hit pretty hard. The can wobbled and the ball ricocheted down the hall.

More wild laughter erupted from the group.

Arthur couldn't figure out why a cafeteria garbage can would be sitting in the hallway. Or why the jocks would be gathered around it, laughing and whipping basketballs at it.

Until he saw the top of somebody's head appear.

TWENTY-TWO

Arthur couldn't remember exactly what he'd yelled at the group. He thought it was something like "Stop it, what are you doing?" with maybe a couple of swearwords added in.

It was called a fight, but it really wasn't.

The jocks said Arthur threw his books as he ran toward them. They said he tried to kill them with his *Great Works of Literature* textbook and with the large and deadly U.S. history textbooks he was carrying, which could kill just about anyone.

This was not true.

Arthur did not throw his books. He dropped them as he got closer because he wanted to have his hands free to defend himself. He had learned a few things in juvie.

He might have dropped the textbooks with more force than he needed to because he thought the slam of the books would get the guys' attention and make them take off. (In hindsight, a pretty idiotic idea.) But he wasn't dumb enough to throw anything at anybody again.

Arthur ran toward the guys with only one thought in mind, really: Saving whoever was in the garbage can. Or at least getting the person out.

Normally, Arthur wasn't the saving type. He wasn't sure why this scene bothered him as much as it did. If it hadn't been for his probation sentence, maybe he wouldn't have noticed the kid in the garbage can at all. Or maybe it was some leftover guilt about what he'd done to the Junk Man still hanging around.

Whatever the reason, this weird burst of anger came over Arthur when he saw what was happening. Did the jocks think it was funny to throw someone in a trash can? Was it some kind of prank?

Without thinking much about the consequences, he rushed toward the group. His long legs churned up the distance. He was a decent runner when he was angry.

"Look out for the juvie freak!" the jocks laughed as they backed toward the sides of the hallway, leaving the garbage can behind like an abandoned island in the middle of the hall.

Stupidly, Arthur didn't pay much attention to where the guys went. All he cared about was that they'd left the person inside the garbage can alone. When he got to it, he peered into the shadowy depths, not knowing what to expect.

A pale, round face surrounded by a lot of other round faces stared up at him.

It took Arthur a minute to realize that only one round

face was a kid's. The others were basketballs. The kid had been dumped into one of the big trash cans of balls from the gym.

"Want to play some ball?" the kid said, trying to smile as he looked up.

Arthur could tell he'd been crying. He had smeary square glasses that looked way too fragile and professor-like. Glasses that seemed to say *Please beat me up*.

"What are you doing in there?" Arthur snapped. As if the kid had a choice.

"I don't know." The boy's eyes blinked fast behind his glasses.

"Well, stand up and I'll help you get out," Arthur said, feeling more irritated as time went on. He was mad at everything—the nerdy kid, the jocks, himself for getting involved.

Because the trash can was so big, it was a struggle to get the short kid over the side and onto the floor again. Finally, Arthur had to half lift him out by his armpits, which was embarrassing—especially since he was pretty sure the boy was a seventh grader like he was.

Once the kid's feet were safely on the ground—feet that were wearing polished brown loafers, by the way—Arthur couldn't help shoving the trash can toward the wall where some of the jocks were standing. Just to pay them back. Because brown-loafer, gold-glasses kid probably never would.

This was a mistake.

Of course, the can tipped over and basketballs went

rolling everywhere. And one of the jocks behind Arthur took the opportunity created by the chaos to ram him into the wall of lockers. (Arthur didn't see what happened to gold-glasses kid.)

And of course, this was the moment when the varsity coaches and various other official people arrived.

Nobody needed to tackle Arthur, because he was already sprawled on the linoleum. Without asking him why he was there, or letting him explain anything, they hauled him away to the office, one red-faced, huffing coach on each side.

Arthur figured Officer Billie would probably count this as messing up. Big-time.

TWENTY-THREE

The kid was called Squeak.

Arthur remembered that as he sat in the office. Squeak had been in one of his classes back in elementary school. He couldn't recall the kid's real name. Arthur figured everybody called him Squeak because of his size, but he wasn't sure. He knew he'd never talked to him before.

Why had he gotten involved?

Arthur shook his head, more annoyed with himself than anyone else. He already had enough problems.

The door of the vice principal's office opened up on Arthur's left. He forced himself not to look. Let Vice make the first move. Let Vice speak to him first.

Squeak came out of the office and passed Arthur. He could hear the faint creak of his leather loafers and a snuffling sound that he assumed was the tail end of the kid's crying. He was a real shrimp for a seventh grader, Arthur noticed again, feeling bad for his nonexistent hormones.

Squeak didn't say anything to Arthur. He slipped into the noisy hall like some kind of invisible spirit.

"Mr. Owens." Vice stood in the doorway of his office, arms folded. "You're next."

Vice's small, windowless office smelled of stale coffee and body odor.

"Sit down, Mr. Owens." Vice pointed to one of the leather chairs by his desk. Arthur slid into it, careful not to make eye contact with Vice, careful not to think the chairs were nice.

"Well," Vice said. "We've had quite a day today, haven't we, Mr. Owens?"

Arthur shrugged and mumbled, "Guess so."

Vice leaned back, twisting and untwisting a paper clip with his fingers. "Although I find this very hard to believe, Reginald says you were not one of the instigators today. Is that correct?"

The kid's real name was *Reginald*?

Jeez. Arthur tried not to shake his head at the bad luck the kid had. Abnormally short. Gold glasses. And a name like Reginald.

"I'm waiting on an answer," Vice said. "Spit it out. I don't have all day."

"I was just trying to help," Arthur replied sullenly, still looking down at the floor. "That's all."

"And by 'help' you mean what?"

Arthur shrugged again. "Just getting him out of the trash can. What else?"

"So you go around *helping* people all the time, do you?" Vice said sarcastically.

"Maybe," Arthur retorted.

Vice tossed the deformed paper clip onto his desk. Arthur heard the tiny ping of it landing. "Here's what I have a problem with, Mr. Owens: You are a convicted felon. You've been in jail. . . ."

Arthur kept his eyes on the office floor. He pictured all of the layers of cement, dirt, rocks, magma, and continental plates below his feet as Vice went on talking. He couldn't be bothered to correct the vice principal's lies. It didn't matter, he told himself. Let people believe what they wanted.

"From what I can gather, Reginald is the only one who says you were helping him," Vice continued. "Every other person in the hallway says they saw you tormenting him—putting him in the garbage can and throwing balls at him."

Arthur's eyes shot upward. "Well, they're wrong."

"Here's what I think." Vice leaned forward. "I think Reginald is afraid of you and is afraid to give me the truth. And let me tell you." Vice pointed at Arthur. "If I see you lay one finger on him again—one finger—I'm calling your probation officer and you are out of this school for good. You stay away from Reginald. Do you understand me?"

"Yes," Arthur said. In his head, he replied, *Loud and clear.*

He left Vice's office and went back to class.

But apparently nobody gave Squeak the message about staying away from Arthur, because the next day at lunch, Squeak sat down next to him.

THE SECOND IMPORTANT THING

"What are you doing?" Arthur said when Squeak pulled out the chair next to him.

"Can I sit at your table?" the kid asked, his eyes blinking nervously behind his old-man glasses. He was wearing a plaid shirt and a bow tie. He carried a carton of white milk and a neatly folded lunch bag.

Are you kidding me? Arthur thought.

"No," he replied, shaking his head. "You can't. Find somewhere else."

"Why?"

"Because Vice says I'm dangerous and I'm supposed to stay away from you. So take off and find another table."

"Good," the kid said, sliding into the seat next to Arthur. "Dangerous is good." He reached out his hand as if they were at a formal event. "Hello, I'm Reggie, but everybody calls me Squeak. Pleased to meet you."

Arthur ignored the pale, outstretched hand and went back to scarfing down the soggy hamburger on his tray. "Seriously, you need to sit somewhere else," he repeated. "I'm not going through all that crap with Vice again."

"There's no law against sitting where you want in the cafeteria," the kid insisted.

Arthur snorted. "Right. Vice says there is."

"Well, he's wrong. And if he says anything about it, I'll tell him he's wrong." Squeak pulled his seat closer to the table and seemed determined not to move, no matter what. "So your name is Arthur Owens?" he asked, changing the subject.

"Yeah."

"You're in seventh grade too?"

"Yeah." Arthur tried to say as little as possible, in the hopes that Squeak would get the hint and leave.

"Well, I want to thank you for what you did yesterday," Squeak continued in his polite, professor-like voice. "I'm sorry you had to get into a fight like that."

"It wasn't a fight. I just scared the guys off. No big deal." Arthur shoved the rest of his hamburger into his mouth and began to clean up his spot at the table. He didn't owe Squeak anything. If he wanted to stay there and sit at the table by himself, fine.

It was Squeak's lunch that made him stop.

Squeak had just opened his brown bag and started to set his lunch on the table. What caught Arthur's attention wasn't what he had brought for lunch; it was the fact that everything Squeak pulled out of his bag—except the white paper napkin—was precisely and perfectly wrapped in Most Important Thing #2.

Foil.

"My mother likes everything to be neat," Squeak said, noticing Arthur's stare as he unwrapped each item. A sandwich, an apple, and a roll of vanilla creme cookies. "What can I say?" He gave an embarrassed smile. "She still makes my lunch."

Arthur didn't know what to think. The connection with Mr. Hampton's list was too bizarre.

"I know it's weird," Squeak said sheepishly. "I know I should make my own lunch. Maybe I'll start doing that." He took a small bite of his sandwich and glanced nervously at Arthur. "Are you upset about something else?"

Arthur hesitated before saying, "No, it's just—well, I work for this guy who sometimes collects foil."

Squeak pushed the clump of discarded foil pieces toward Arthur. "Well, here, you can give him a gift from me. And there's lots more where that came from, don't worry." He gave one of his goofy, too-wide grins. "I bring the same lunch to school every day: A ham and cheese sandwich. One apple or orange. And six cookies—usually vanilla cremes, sometimes Oreos. Always wrapped in foil. Hasn't changed since kindergarten."

The bell rang before Squeak finished the last of his cookies.

He shoved the rest inside his lunch bag. "So tomorrow, I'll

be here again, okay?" Squeak said quickly as he jumped up. "You'll be here too, right?" He gave Arthur a worried look.

"Sure," Arthur replied, because he was still kind of stunned.

"Okay, see you tomorrow." Squeak waved and scurried away.

TWENTY-FOUR

They kept eating lunch together. Arthur wasn't sure why. Partly he didn't want to hurt Squeak's feelings, and partly he felt like it might be bad luck to stop. He couldn't explain why Squeak and the foil were important, but he felt that somehow they were. If nothing else, Squeak's lunches saved him a lot of work on Saturdays. He didn't have to scrounge around in people's garbage cans looking for foil anymore.

One lunch period, he wrote out the list of the Seven Most Important Things while Squeak was finishing his usual foil-wrapped lineup of sandwich, apple, and cookies. If anybody could figure out what Mr. Hampton's list meant, Arthur thought, it would be Squeak—who was abnormally smart about everything. He took courses like Algebra I and chemistry that Arthur didn't even know seventh graders could take.

"Here. I've got something for you to look at," Arthur said, passing the sheet of notebook paper across the table. "What do you think the things on this list mean?"

Squeak straightened his glasses and studied the page. "You mean, what do they have in common?"

"Sure. Yeah."

"Do you want to know the spelling error you made too?"

Arthur scowled. "No."

"Okay, just asking," Squeak answered quickly. "I wasn't sure if it was an assignment for class or not." He tilted his head from one side to the other, looking at the list silently. Then turned the paper upside down. And then right side up again. "Is this a trick question?" he asked finally.

"No."

Squeak chewed on his lip and squinted at the paper. "I can see only a couple of things they have in common. First, from a scientific standpoint, they're all solids."

Arthur gave a sarcastic snort. "So are your cookies. And this table." He glanced toward the administrators standing nearby. "And Vice's brain."

"You didn't ask me about Vice's brain," Squeak retorted. "You asked me about your list." After looking at the paper for a long time again, he continued, "Okay, this one is kind of vague. Cardboard boxes, coffee cans, bottles, foil—they all hold things."

"Mirrors?"

"Your reflection."

"Oh yeah," said Arthur, thinking that was kind of a stretch.

"Third, everything except cardboard and wood is shiny or reflective."

Great. Squeak was one of the smartest kids in the school, and that's the best he could come up with? He was collecting shiny solid stuff that held things—so what?

"What's the list from?" Squeak asked curiously.

Arthur took one of Squeak's vanilla creme cookies because he never ate all of them. "They're from my probation."

Squeak looked confused. "Foil and cardboard are your probation?"

"Yeah," Arthur said, shoving the cookie into his mouth. "I collect them for the guy I threw the brick at."

Then he glanced uneasily at Squeak, wondering if maybe he didn't know the whole story—although that seemed impossible. *Everybody* at Byrd Junior High knew the whole story. "You know I threw a brick at a guy, right?"

Looking uncomfortable, Squeak nodded. "Yes, I heard that's what you did."

"Well," Arthur continued, "he was a homeless guy who used to go around my neighborhood collecting junk. Everybody called him the Junk Man. For my probation, I work for him every Saturday, collecting stuff off this list—"

"And that's why you take the foil from my lunch," Squeak interrupted.

"Exactly."

"Does the list ever change?"

Arthur shook his head. "No, it's always these same things. You can't substitute anything else. If you leave him a lamp instead of a lightbulb, he flips out. He collects wings too," he added, thinking of his dad's hat. "And I used to see him picking up wine bottles and other junk when I was a kid."

Squeak tilted his head, studying the list again. "Is it possible he uses them for building or making something? Or inventing something?"

"Old coffee cans and empty wine bottles?"

"I don't know." Squeak folded up the list and passed it back to Arthur. "Of course, there's always the possibility he could be an enigma," he added.

"Enigma?"

"Someone who doesn't make sense. Maybe you are collecting an enigmatic list for an enigmatic person," Squeak replied in this superior tone that really ticked Arthur off sometimes. So the kid was a genius. Who cared? He was about to tell Squeak to stop being a jerk when the bell rang.

"I'll keep thinking," Squeak said as he scooped up his lunch garbage. "Maybe I'll come up with something."

"Don't bother," Arthur called over his shoulder as he took off.

TWENTY-FIVE

And then, as if to prove Arthur wrong, the list changed.

It was the first Saturday in February. A sunny, almost-warm day. In a lot of places, you could spot some patches of almost-green grass showing.

When Arthur arrived at Hampton's garage, he expected to find the same cardboard note with the same list. It was his seventh Saturday of work, and nothing had changed so far. In fact, he almost didn't bother to read what was written on the sign attached to the grocery cart. Only a moron wouldn't have the seven most important things memorized by now.

Fortunately, he glanced at the sign and noticed that it was new, and it had only one item listed this time. In the same square printing as the other signs, it said: ARTUR—FIND THRONE CHAIR.

What? Arthur thought, rereading the note. Where in the

world did Mr. Hampton think he would find a *throne* in this run-down neighborhood?

He looked around at the leaning telephone poles, the rusted chain-link fences, the crooked porches. Most of the houses didn't even have a decent chair on the front porch, let alone a throne.

Or was it a misspelling? Did he actually mean a *thrown-out* chair?

That seemed more likely, especially since Mr. Hampton still misspelled Arthur's name on every sign.

Surprisingly enough, chairs weren't that hard to find in the trash on Saturdays. People seemed to get rid of chairs a lot. Most weekends, you could usually find a couple of saggy sofas waiting by the curb too.

At least Mr. Hampton hadn't asked him to get a sofa. Arthur grinned. That would have been a real treat to get in a grocery cart.

It didn't take long for him to spot the first possible chair candidate, a few houses away from the garage. It was a metal desk chair with one broken armrest and rusted legs. Not great, but he thought it might work if he got desperate.

On the next street, he found a nice blue plaid armchair. It had some puffs of loose stuffing coming out of its cushions, but the rest of it seemed to be in good shape. The main problem for Arthur was how to get the big chair into the cart without killing himself.

After trying—and failing—to lift the thing, he decided he'd stop back for it later if he couldn't find anything else.

Toward the end of his four hours, he came upon the red-and-gold masterpiece.

It was sitting outside a rambling two-story Victorian house that looked like a decrepit museum. Arthur figured they must have been cleaning out the place, because there were rolls of carpet and rusty sinks and old light fixtures and lots of other trash piled by the curb. But what caught his eye was the big chair sitting on top of the haphazard pile.

Wow—a throne was his first thought.

The chair was covered in red velvet fabric that was stained and worn in a lot of places, but you could tell it had probably been an expensive chair once. Its heavy wooden arms and wide back were carved with swirls and decorations that had been painted in thick layers of metallic gold. One of the front legs was missing and a lot of the paint was flaking, but if you squinted, it could definitely be a throne.

Without a doubt, Arthur knew this was the chair Mr. Hampton wanted.

The trick was how to get the thing onto the cart. It took him forever to figure out how to lift it and balance it on the top of the cart, and then he spent more than an hour slowly pushing it back to the garage. As he was crossing one street, a guy in a pickup truck offered Arthur ten bucks for the thing. "I'll take it off your hands," he said.

Arthur shook his head and kept going.

Two other people stopped to ask if he needed help. One

car full of high school jerks honked and yelled stuff at him. Arthur resisted the urge to make a rude gesture. He just kept staring straight ahead, pretending he'd seen nothing.

When he finally got back to the garage, he left the chair sitting right next to the side door so Hampton wouldn't miss it. He put the sign that said ARTUR—FIND THRONE CHAIR in the middle of the red velvet seat, as if to emphasize that this was it. He'd found the perfect one.

He couldn't wait to see what James Hampton thought of it.

TWENTY-SIX

On the following Saturday, February 8, it was raining. A steady, cold rain. And there were no messages from Mr. Hampton when Arthur arrived. Which was odd.

Arthur was so sure he had found the perfect chair—the perfect throne—for Mr. Hampton that he was kind of disappointed the guy hadn't left a single word to thank him. A little note would have been nice. Especially after all the hassle he'd gone through to haul the chair back to the garage. He thought he should have gotten a few hours deducted from his probation just for that.

Strangely, the shopping cart was missing too.

Arthur walked around outside, carefully stepping over the piles of old concrete blocks and junk, looking for the cart.

He wasn't sure what to do. Mr. Hampton had never forgotten to leave him an assignment before, no matter what the weather was—and he'd collected junk for the guy in a lot worse weather than this.

On his second walk around the building, Arthur happened to notice that the side door of the garage was slightly open. Just a small crack.

That was strange, he thought. It had never been open before. Had Mr. Hampton forgotten to lock it? Or did the open door mean he was supposed to go in?

Something about the open door made him nervous. There was no sign of anyone else around. He couldn't see any lights on inside. He couldn't hear anyone working.

He glanced toward Groovy Jim's shop, wondering if he should go and ask him for help. But Groovy Jim had a customer—a rare occurrence—and he didn't want to bother him. Plus, he thought it would sound kind of crazy if he interrupted someone's tattoo to say he was jumpy about a missing shopping cart and an open door. It was eleven o'clock on a Saturday morning, not midnight, for cripes' sake.

Arthur decided he would knock on the side door and call out for Mr. Hampton. If the guy wasn't there, or didn't answer, he'd go home and let Officer Billie know that nobody had been around. He hoped he'd still get credit for his four hours and hadn't slogged around in the pouring rain for nothing.

Taking a deep breath, Arthur rapped his knuckles on the doorframe and shouted through the dark opening, "Hey, Mr. Hampton, it's Arthur Owens out here. It's Saturday. Can I help you with anything today?"

He knew it sounded really dumb, but he didn't know what else to say. It was how his mom always answered the phone at the dentist's office when he called her. *Hello, this is Linda at Dr. Driscoll's office. Can I help you with anything today?*

Honestly, he wasn't expecting a reply to his question. But right after he said "Can I help you with anything today?" there was a noise inside the garage. It sounded as if a can—or something metallic—had suddenly hit the floor.

Arthur backed away from the door. He could feel his heart speed up. Was there something in there?

He glanced around for an object to use as a weapon if he needed it. A plank of wood with a couple of rusty nails sticking out of it lay on the ground nearby. He picked it up gingerly and used it to push the door open a little wider, thinking maybe whatever was inside would come running out.

Nothing did.

There was an old paint can lid next to his feet, he noticed. Just to see what would happen, he picked it up and tossed it into the darkness. He could hear the lid rolling and spinning across what must have been a cement floor.

Again, nothing.

Arthur took another deep breath, telling himself he was thirteen years old and should have more guts. He had survived three weeks in juvie with Slash. He'd gone up against half of the varsity football team at his school to rescue Squeak from the trash can. It was ridiculous to be scared of a garage in the middle of the day.

Still holding the piece of nail-studded wood, Arthur eased cautiously through the doorway. His wet shoes squelched on the cement, which was the only sound—other than his heart pounding in his ears—he could hear at first.

Silently, he searched along the side of the doorframe for a light switch. He was sure there must be one nearby—especially if Mr. Hampton worked there late at night, which Groovy Jim said he did sometimes. The old guy wouldn't wander around blindly in the dark.

Arthur's fingers finally found the switch next to the door.

Instinctively, he squinted before pushing the switch upward, as if expecting it to be painfully bright, like suddenly going from a dark room into the blazing sunlight.

But he definitely wasn't prepared for the dazzling vision that awaited him.

TWENTY-SEVEN

All Arthur saw at first was a wall of gold and silver. A stunned gasp escaped from him.

What the heck had he stumbled upon?

It looked like a shimmering shrine inside the garage, like something you'd see on a Hollywood movie set or in an Egyptian temple or something. There were glittering tables, silver pillars, gilt pedestals, and throne-like chairs. Arthur couldn't believe his eyes. Radiant gold-and-silver objects filled almost half of the room—the pieces piled so high they nearly touched the low ceiling lights.

It was *unreal.*

Arthur wondered if he was having a hallucination or some kind of crazy dream. Was he really standing inside Mr. Hampton's garage in Washington, D.C.? He closed his eyes and opened them again just to check if everything was still there.

It was.

And that's when he noticed something else.

There were wings *everywhere*. They were attached to the sides of the tables, the backs of the chairs, the pedestals and pillars. Everything he could see had its own pair of sparkling wings.

Arthur remembered what Mr. Hampton had said about his dad's hat. *I took it for the wings.*

Was this what he'd meant?

Still trying to grasp the unbelievable scene in front of him, Arthur stood motionless by the door. His leaky boots made two moist prints like wings on the cement. Where had Mr. Hampton found all of these things? And what was the mysterious creation supposed to be?

Arthur might have stayed frozen in the same spot forever, lost in the vision of the shimmering world, if it hadn't been for the sound.

From the opposite side of the garage, Arthur heard a low moan.

His eyes darted toward the far corner of the garage, where there didn't seem to be much light—only pools of darkness and shadow, and piles of stuff he couldn't really identify in the gloom. Except for one thing.

A man lying on the floor.

He wore a familiar tan coat. His shoes were still on his feet, and a pair of shattered glasses rested on the floor in front of his head.

Arthur's heart dropped.

James Hampton.

TWENTY-EIGHT

Later on, Arthur couldn't remember everything that happened. It was like the night his dad died. He could only recall certain sights and sounds: the rain on the officers' shoulders, the word *instantly*. . . .

Arthur remembered running over to James Hampton and picking up his broken glasses from the cement floor. He remembered the bitter smell of urine and vomit around him. And he remembered crouching down next to the old man, desperately praying, begging, hoping he was still alive.

"Who are you?" Mr. Hampton said, suddenly opening his eyes and scaring the heck out of Arthur.

"A-Arthur Owens," he stammered.

The man's dark eyes looked distant and unfocused, as if they didn't actually see Arthur but someone else. "I don't know you," he mumbled. "Tell me where I am, saint."

Arthur swallowed, unsure what to answer. "Your garage,"

he replied finally. "And I'm not a saint," he added. "I'm Arthur Owens, the kid doing the probation sentence for you."

He couldn't bring himself to mention the brick.

"Oh yes, Saint Arthur," the man murmured, his eyes sliding closed again. "Now I know exactly who you are. You're the one who saved me."

"I didn't save you," Arthur started to explain, but stopped when he saw Mr. Hampton's closed eyes and rasping breaths. He could feel panic rising in his throat. He didn't know if Mr. Hampton had fallen or had a heart attack or what. With his face crumpled against the cold cement floor, the old man looked like he was dying.

Arthur glanced toward the side door of the garage, desperately hoping someone would arrive. If Mr. Hampton died while he was there, nobody would believe it wasn't his fault.

But no one came.

Arthur shook the old man's shoulder, begging him to wake up.

"Can you hear me, Mr. Hampton? I have to go and get some help for you, okay?" Arthur's panicked voice echoed through the garage, but the man didn't move or answer. At the other end of the room, the dozens of gold-and-silver wings remained motionless too. Nothing stirred.

Arthur felt as if he was about to explode with fear. He was afraid to stay with Mr. Hampton, and he was afraid to leave.

He'd already deserted Mr. Hampton once. He'd left him lying alone on a city sidewalk and run away like a coward. If he left to get help, would he look like a coward again?

Arthur decided he had to take the chance. He couldn't stay there and watch the guy die. Standing up, he took one last look at the motionless man and ran to get Groovy Jim.

The rest of what happened was a blur to Arthur. He remembered bursting into Groovy Jim's shop, shouting things that probably didn't make much sense, about finding Mr. Hampton on the floor and calling the police. He remembered Groovy Jim running up the gravel alley in his slippers, with his burly customer following him. And he remembered almost crying with relief when Groovy Jim kneeled down next to Mr. Hampton and he opened his eyes again.

"What happened to you, buddy?" Groovy Jim said, trying to sound calm as he tucked the man's coat tighter around him and patted his arm. "You take a fall and hit your head or something?"

"No." Mr. Hampton's head moved almost imperceptibly. "I'm ready to go," he whispered.

"Go where?" Groovy Jim asked, just to keep him talking, Arthur could tell.

"Heaven," replied Mr. Hampton, closing his eyes again.

Looking startled, Groovy Jim glanced back at Arthur and his customer. "Well, I don't think heaven is ready for you yet, buddy," he said loudly. "You need to stay right here with us until help gets here. You've got a lot of years left to live. You can't get rid of us that easily."

He pointed toward the dazzling display at the other end

of the garage. "Man, that's a pretty cool collection of stuff you've got over there. Why don't you tell us about it?"

Surprisingly, this question seemed to bring James Hampton back to the real world again. His eyes opened and he focused them directly on Groovy Jim. "Not *stuff*," he corrected, sounding irritated. "It's heaven. Saint Arthur and I have been busy building heaven."

Groovy Jim's eyes darted toward Arthur, who stared at Hampton uneasily. *What in the world was the guy talking about?*

"I've been helping you collect junk, remember?" he blurted out, as if that might jog Mr. Hampton's memory. "Remember the list of the Seven Most Important Things? Foil, cardboard, glass . . ." He stumbled through the simple list of items he'd been collecting since December.

"Exactly," James Hampton said, sliding his gaze slowly toward Arthur. "What else do you think heaven would be made out of?"

TWENTY-NINE

All the way to the hospital, Arthur kept thinking about what Mr. Hampton had said.

It seemed like forever before the ambulance had arrived for him. Once Mr. Hampton had been loaded into it, Arthur got into one of the cop cars to ride along to the hospital. Groovy Jim stayed behind to finish working on his customer.

"You sure you don't mind going by yourself?" Groovy Jim had asked before Arthur left.

He nodded, even though he wasn't really okay with it. He had no idea what he was supposed to do once they got to the hospital. Or how he'd get home. He didn't even have a dime to call someone.

When the cop got into the car, he turned to Arthur and said, "Bet this is your first ride in a police car, isn't it, kid?"

Arthur said, "Yeah."

He resisted adding that it was his first ride without handcuffs, anyhow.

As the officer backed the car down the alley and sped down the block, siren blaring, Arthur kept going over and over in his mind what James Hampton had said.

Had he really made all the gold and silver pieces in the garage himself? And had he really meant they were supposed to look like *heaven*—the place—with angels and pearly gates and all that?

After his dad died, Arthur had spent a lot of time thinking about heaven. Wondering if it was real and what it was like. Wondering if his dad was there—despite what his stupid aunt had said at the funeral home.

Sometimes in juvie when he couldn't sleep, he would try to picture the perfect heaven for his dad. He would imagine a place full of motorcycles and lots of things to fix, because his dad always liked to tinker with stuff. A place that was sunny and warm year-round, so his dad would never have to put his Harley away.

Mostly, he pictured heaven being kind of like Florida with motorcycles.

But he'd never imagined finding heaven in a garage in Washington, D.C.

He still couldn't quite believe what he'd seen. Had the whole thing really been made of junk he'd collected?

Arthur closed his eyes, trying to recall what the arrangement had looked like. He hadn't gotten a good look at the pieces, but it didn't seem possible that the fancy tables and chairs and pillars were made of stuff from the trash. Nobody was that good an artist.

But there were all those wings. How could you explain

the wings? Mr. Hampton had taken his father's hat *for the wings,* and he'd signed all his notes St. James. The grocery cart was a chariot, Hampton had told Arthur's sister. The week before, he'd sent Arthur to find a throne.

Thrones, chariots, wings, saints . . . heaven?

Arthur shook his head.

It made sense—and didn't make any sense, at the same time.

But the more puzzling question was why.

Why was Hampton building heaven? And—Arthur glanced anxiously over his shoulder at the ambulance screaming through the rain behind them—what if Hampton died before he found out?

THIRTY

They wheeled James Hampton through the whooshing doors of the emergency department, and a young nurse took Arthur to the waiting room. Arthur wasn't sure what happened to the cop, but he never returned after dropping him off at the door.

"We'll come and get you once we have him stabilized," the nurse said kindly as she steered Arthur toward a row of empty seats. She reminded him of a pretty nurse you'd see on television. "What's your name?"

"Arthur Owens."

"Is the man they brought in a friend of yours?"

"No," Arthur replied uncomfortably. "He's just someone I help out sometimes." He knew this sounded kind of weird, but what else could he say?

The nurse pressed her lips together, as if this wasn't the answer she was hoping for. She seemed unsure of what to do next, and Arthur wondered if maybe she hadn't been on the job very long. "Do you know if he has any family we could contact?"

Arthur shook his head, remembering what Mr. Hampton had told his sister: No kids. No house. "I don't think so."

"Okay." The nurse patted Arthur's shoulder, making him feel even more embarrassed. "We'll see what we can find out, don't worry. Can I get you some juice or cookies while you're waiting? We have some in the back."

Arthur wanted to say yes. His throat felt like the Sahara. His stomach grumbled. It seemed like hours since he'd left home that morning.

Despite this, he heard himself answer, "No, I'm fine. Thanks." He didn't know why he had to appear tough and strong in front of the nurse, but he did.

"All right." The nurse smiled at him, and Arthur could tell his face was getting warmer. "Just sit tight and I'll let you know when we have some news, okay?"

Arthur watched the nurse turn and disappear through a set of doors marked STAFF ONLY as if she were his last connection to the outside world. He'd never been in a hospital by himself before.

Sagging into one of the uncomfortable chairs, he gazed around the waiting room. It had a pay phone, two small televisions showing only static, and a magazine rack with almost no magazines in it. The people in the room looked like they had been there for weeks.

Some people dozed, leaning on their arms. A few read.

Arthur had no idea what to do. He was miles away from his neighborhood, with no way of telling anyone where he was. He wished he had Squeak's phone number. At least Squeak would have been someone to talk to.

"Peppermint?" An old woman with rumpled hair and a lint-covered coat leaned toward him, holding a piece of striped candy in her hand.

Arthur shook his head. "No thanks." He didn't want to make friends with anybody here, or for anyone to try to make friends with him.

There were no clocks in the waiting room. Arthur had no idea how much time passed before the same nurse finally came back to get him. All he knew was that his head was pounding and he felt a little dizzy when he stood up.

"He's doing better now, so you can see him for a few minutes," the nurse said as she led him down a hallway where he was the only nonmedical person around. "He called you a saint for saving him." She glanced at Arthur over her shoulder. "Isn't that sweet?"

"Yeah—yeah, he calls a lot of people that," Arthur stammered, hoping that was all Mr. Hampton had told the nurse about him.

"Well, you got him here in time. That's the main thing." She gave Arthur another one of her dazzling smiles, and he couldn't imagine how a person this nice could also stick people with needles.

"Is he going to be okay?" Arthur asked, because it seemed like something he ought to ask, even though he didn't know Mr. Hampton that well—or at all, really.

"I'll let him talk to you," the nurse answered. "And here we are." She stopped by a green curtain.

Arthur couldn't help noticing how the curtain was the same shade of olive-green as the uniforms they had in juvie.

"Mr. Hampton, I have a visitor to see you," the nurse called out before they entered. "It's the saint you were asking about," she added, giving Arthur a wink.

"Well, bring him in," a shaky voice replied.

The nurse pushed the curtain aside, and Arthur took a deep breath to calm down before he stepped into the small space—trying not to be afraid, trying not to look afraid.

He had no idea what to expect. Until he'd found Mr. Hampton on the floor of the garage that morning, Arthur hadn't seen him face to face since the day in the courtroom. He wasn't even sure he was *allowed* to be face to face with him.

When Arthur came in, Mr. Hampton was propped up in a hospital bed, covered in blankets. He didn't resemble the neat, brown-suited man from the courtroom or the crazy Junk Man either. Mostly, he looked tired and old. His skin reminded Arthur of the cardboard he'd been collecting for months—but cardboard that had been left out in the rain. Rain-soaked and sagging cardboard. That was what Arthur thought at first.

Mr. Hampton lifted his hand from the blankets in a small

wave, and Arthur noticed for the first time that he was no longer wearing the cast and sling on his arm. "So, we meet again," the old man said with a weak smile.

"Yes." Arthur nodded, shifting uncomfortably from one foot to the other. He tried not to look at all the tubes and wires around the man. "Are you feeling better?" he asked, hoping it wasn't an impolite question, hoping his voice wasn't too loud in the small space. Mr. Hampton wasn't deaf, he reminded himself. Just sick.

"*Better* is a relative term," the man replied with a tired sigh. "I'm better than I was an hour ago, but not as good as I used to be."

Arthur wasn't sure if he should ask him what was wrong. Fortunately, a buzzer in the hallway interrupted the conversation.

"You can visit for a little while longer, if you'd like," the nurse told Arthur. "I need to leave for a minute, but I'll take you to the waiting room once I get back." She pointed to a red buzzer near the bed. "There's an alarm if you need anything, Mr. Hampton, okay?"

Arthur was relieved that the nurse talked extra loudly to him too.

After the nurse left, Mr. Hampton motioned to Arthur. "Come here and let me shake your hand, young man."

Arthur was startled. Didn't the guy remember who he was and what he'd done?

"I won't bite," the old man said, waving again.

Reluctantly, Arthur stepped toward the bed. For some

reason, it seemed wrong to shake hands with the man he'd almost killed. He half expected a big lightning bolt to come down and zap him, or the police to barge in and arrest him on the spot.

But it was just an ordinary handshake. For as tired as he looked, Mr. Hampton's grip was still pretty strong, Arthur noticed.

"I want to thank you for saving me twice," Mr. Hampton said, pulling himself higher on the pillows and rearranging the blankets.

Arthur was confused. "Twice?"

"The brick?" the old man said with a sharp look. "Surely you haven't forgotten that?"

Arthur swallowed. "No."

"Well, that was the first time you saved me."

What? Arthur thought maybe Mr. Hampton didn't re-member exactly what had happened. "No, I was the one who threw the brick that hit you in the shoulder," he tried to ex-plain. "You fell on the sidewalk and broke your arm. Then someone else stopped and helped you, remember?"

"Nope. That's where you're wrong, young man," Mr. Hampton replied in a determined voice. "I needed assistance with my project, and your brick falling out of the sky and breaking my arm is what brought the two of us together. That way, I could keep building my masterpiece while you collected the Seven Most Important Things for me. So it was *you* who saved me."

Arthur shook his head slowly. The guy was nuts.

"It's true," Mr. Hampton insisted. He stuck two fingers in

the air. "Second time you saved me—this morning. I could've been lying there for days if it hadn't been for you finding me." The old man closed his eyes. "Twice. Like I said."

"Okay," replied Arthur, feeling a little guilty for agreeing with the guy. But he didn't know what else to do. He knew he hadn't thrown the brick to help anybody—especially not Mr. Hampton.

After a minute or two of silence, the man's eyes opened again. "So, how much do you know about my work?"

"Uh, not much," Arthur mumbled, wondering how much he could know about it. He'd only seen it once—that morning.

"Well, I'm building the Throne of the Third Heaven."

"All right." Arthur nodded politely, as if building heaven was a perfectly normal thing to do. He didn't dare ask how many heavens and thrones there were altogether—or how Mr. Hampton knew he was building the third one.

"Have you ever met an artist who was creating heaven?"

Arthur had to admit he hadn't.

"That's because almost no one else has done it," Mr. Hampton said. "You can do your own research if you want to. Go to the library. Look it up. Lots of people have done hell. Hell is easy to create."

Arthur figured that was probably true. He could probably do a decent drawing of what hell was like, based on the past year of his life.

"Heaven—that's a whole different ball game," Mr. Hampton continued. "It takes years. A lifetime. I have a lot left to do."

Arthur couldn't help remembering how just a few hours earlier, Mr. Hampton had been saying he wanted to die. He was glad the guy seemed to have changed his mind.

"But now I'm stuck here." The man waved one arm in the air, looking irritated by his surroundings.

There was a pause. Arthur could hear people going past in the hallway. Buzzers hummed and beeped in the distance. It was a strange place to be having a conversation about heaven and hell, he thought.

Mr. Hampton's dark eyes scrutinized Arthur. "So can I trust you to keep collecting things while I'm gone?"

"I guess," Arthur replied, not sounding very sure. "The same seven things?"

"Of course." Mr. Hampton gave Arthur an odd look. "They're the building blocks of heaven."

"Yeah. Okay." Arthur nodded, as if this made complete sense. Cardboard and coffee cans and lightbulbs were the building blocks of heaven. Everyone knew that.

"You can leave whatever you collect inside the garage," the old man continued. "But don't move anything while I'm gone. Everything has its place and is exactly where it should be. Is that clear?"

Arthur nodded again.

Suddenly looking exhausted, Mr. Hampton sighed. "Who knows when I'll get out of here. Until then"—he pointed to a set of keys resting on the bedside table— "there are the keys to the garage, so you can keep an eye on my masterpiece for me." He closed his eyes. "Thank you for coming to visit, Saint Arthur. I need to rest now. See you later."

Arthur picked up the keys reluctantly. He wasn't sure whether to correct Mr. Hampton about the Saint Arthur part of what he'd said or not.

"Wait. Hold on."

Eyes still closed, Mr. Hampton held up one hand in a way that reminded Arthur exactly of Officer Billie. "I forgot to thank you for the very nice throne you found last week. It was perfect. Also . . . ," he continued, "I asked the nurse about spare coffee cans and foil, and she said they might have some in the hospital cafeteria, so make sure you check with her before you leave."

"Okay," Arthur agreed as he slipped around the curtain, although there was no way—*no way*—he was going to ask the pretty nurse for any leftover garbage from the cafeteria. Even saints had their limits.

Outside the room, the hallway was busy. The nurse spotted Arthur as he made the mistake of turning right down the hall instead of left.

"The waiting area is this way," she said, pointing. "How did your visit with your friend go?"

Arthur shrugged. "Fine."

"He's still a little confused, I think. But we'll take good care of him, don't worry." She gave Arthur another one of her movie star smiles. He could feel his ears turning beet red. "Can I call someone to pick you up? You've been here a long time by yourself."

Arthur knew his mom wouldn't be home yet. She had made plans to spend the day visiting one of his aunts, and she wouldn't be back until late. Barbara was at a neighbor's house. He didn't have Squeak's phone number either. The only person he could think of calling for a ride home was the last person he really wanted to talk to—Officer Billie.

THIRTY-ONE

Officer Billie showed up at the hospital wearing a pair of white pajamas. At least, that's what Arthur thought at first.

He was in the waiting room with the old lady and all of the other permanent-looking hospital visitors when Officer Billie barreled through the door about an hour after he'd called her. Her dark hair was sticking up in spiky tufts, and a brown purse dangled loosely over her arm.

Arthur was so used to seeing Officer Billie in her precisely creased uniform that he might not have recognized her if it hadn't been for the voice.

"Mr. Owens, there you are," she belted out. "I've been trying to locate you all over the hospital."

Arthur wouldn't have admitted it to anyone—they would have had a field day with it at juvie—but he was sort of glad to see his probation officer.

"Karate," Officer Billie said, explaining her odd outfit as she came over to Arthur. "Saturday classes."

Arthur added this to his very short list of surprising things he'd learned about Officer Billie. She made caramel corn and she did karate.

"Are you all right?" The probation officer studied him with her stern cop gaze. It was like sitting under a lamp. It made Arthur sweat.

"Yeah, kind of."

"What happened?"

As Arthur started to answer, Officer Billie glanced around at the other people in the waiting room, who were desperately trying to seem as if they weren't hanging on every word. *"Wait,"* she said, holding up her hand. "We'll talk outside."

Arthur was surprised to see it was still light out. He felt like it should be way past suppertime, but there were some streaks of pinkish yellow left in the sky. The rain seemed to have stopped. Big puddles filled the parking lot.

"Car's over here." Officer Billie pointed at an old blue Pontiac. "Nothing fancy. No sirens on this one," she said with a joking grin as she opened the door for him.

The car smelled like fast food. Officer Billie had to brush some wrappers and leftover fries off the passenger seat before Arthur sat down. "Let me get the door," she said automatically, closing it with a firm thump.

As they waited in a line of traffic, the officer finally turned to Arthur and said, "Now, let's hear the details."

Arthur kept his eyes focused on the scene outside the car window. "I don't know," he answered truthfully. "Mr. Hampton was on the floor of his garage when I got there this morning. I couldn't tell what happened or how long he'd been there."

He didn't mention what Mr. Hampton had been working on. If Officer Billie didn't already know what the guy was doing, he wasn't going to be the one to tell her. Plus, he wasn't even sure he *could* explain it.

"So you got help and went to the hospital with him?"

Arthur nodded.

"Well, I'm extremely proud of you for being in the right place at the right time," Officer Billie said.

In his mind, Arthur added, *Instead of being in the wrong place at the wrong time, like you usually are.*

"The judge will be pleased to hear what you did for Mr. Hampton today."

Then there was a strange pause. Arthur had the feeling Officer Billie was going to say something else but changed her mind.

"You hungry?" she asked as the light in front of them turned green. "How about a burger or something? My treat."

Arthur didn't want to spend any more time with Officer Billie than necessary, but he knew there wouldn't be any supper at home since his mom was gone. Having eaten nothing for hours, he couldn't bring himself to turn down a burger and fries, no matter who bought them.

"All right, sure," he agreed.

Officer Billie pulled into the parking lot of a small diner. It looked pretty empty. Inside, there were about a dozen tables with red-checkered cloths and a row of worn booths. "We'll take a booth," Officer Billie said to the waitress, who seemed to know her.

She put them in a corner one that could have fit a family of eight. Arthur figured Officer Billie probably brought all of her juvenile delinquents there.

"Order whatever you want," Officer Billie said. "I've already eaten." She told the waitress all she needed was a cup of black coffee.

Arthur didn't want to be greedy. Although he could have polished off about three of the diner's Big Platter specials, all he ordered was a cheeseburger, fries, and a Coke.

Fortunately, everything came pretty quickly.

He was just finishing his meal—carefully scraping up the last globs of ketchup with his fries—when Officer Billie said she had something serious to talk about now that he was done eating.

Right then, Arthur knew he never should have agreed to Officer Billie's offer of a free meal. He'd been on the receiving end of enough bad news to know when more was coming.

Officer Billie sighed and folded her hands in front of her. "I'm not going to sugarcoat it. You know me, I don't sugarcoat things."

Arthur nervously swallowed the last of his watery Coke, as if that would help the sudden dryness in his mouth. He had no idea what to expect.

"All right." Officer Billie cleared her throat. "I didn't want to have to be the one to tell you this, but I think you need to know the truth. Especially after what happened today." She paused and looked at Arthur. "I'm sure you've already guessed that Mr. Hampton is very ill."

No, Arthur thought—he hadn't guessed anything. That morning was the first time he'd actually seen Mr. Hampton since the day in court. But he decided it wasn't a smart idea to share that fact with Officer Billie now, so he stayed quiet and let her keep talking.

"The truth is," the officer continued, "he may not have a lot of time left."

Arthur tried not to jump to the worst conclusions right away. "What do you mean?" he asked carefully.

"Mr. Hampton is dying of cancer. Stomach cancer," Officer Billie said in a voice that reminded Arthur of how the cops had told him about his dad. *Tom Owens died instantly.*

Officer Billie drummed her fingers on the side of her coffee mug. "He told the judge about it, but he didn't want anyone else to know. He didn't want it to affect your sentence. And he especially didn't want you to be told," she added.

Arthur wasn't sure what to say. What went through his mind first was, Why did all of this bad stuff keep happening to him? How could the guy he'd just started to get to know be dying of cancer? What would it mean for his probation and for all the work he'd done for him so far?

"So what's going to happen now?" he asked, feeling kind of stunned. "With everything?"

"Well . . . ," Officer Billie said slowly, "I guess you'll keep working for Mr. Hampton as long as he wants you to."

What? Arthur's eyes darted toward Officer Billie. "You mean until he . . ." He couldn't bring himself to say *dies*.

"No, I'm not saying that exactly. . . ."

"I can't do that," Arthur said quickly. "No matter what the judge says, I can't."

Even if it sounded terrible, there was no way he could be around someone who was dying. He knew it would bring back all the bad memories of his dad's death. The judge couldn't make him do that, could he?

"My father died in a motorcycle crash this past summer, did you know that?" Arthur blurted out. For reasons he couldn't explain, his eyes were starting to sting with tears. Embarrassed, he slid out of the booth and began yanking on his coat. He had to leave—he could hardly see what he was doing.

"Yes," Officer Billie answered calmly. She picked up the check and waved it at the waitress to show she was ready to pay. "I am aware of that fact."

"He hit a tree and died instantly."

"Yes, I'm aware of that."

"I'm not going to go through all that again," Arthur said, his voice rising. "I'm not doing it. Tell the judge he needs to find someone else."

"Okay," said Officer Billie, not showing any emotion at all. "I'll inform the judge of your wishes."

"Seriously, I'm not going back," Arthur shouted over his shoulder as he headed for the door and pushed it open, glad for the darkness, glad for the rain, which was falling again.

THIRTY-TWO

That night, Arthur had another one of his bad dreams about his dad.

In this dream, he had to go around the city collecting empty beer bottles in order to save his father's life.

It wasn't difficult to figure out where this dream came from.

Each time Arthur filled a sack with bottles, he'd bring it to Officer Billie, who would weigh it on a gigantic scale in the courthouse, and each time, she'd squint at the number on the scale, shake her head, and say, "Not enough." Then Arthur would stumble back into the darkness to try and find more.

At the same time he was desperately collecting all of the bottles he could find, police cars were getting closer and closer to the door of his house. So the dream became one of those horrible races against time. Could Arthur collect enough bottles before the police arrived to say his dad was dead?

In the dream, it was a warm and rainy August night—just like the night his dad died. Arthur kept slipping and falling on the slick streets. Bottles kept rolling out of sight and disappearing as he reached for them. Officer Billie kept saying *Not enough, not enough*.

Arthur had a lot of these dreams—dreams where he was trying to save his dad.

They all ended the same way.

He always woke up before he could succeed.

THIRTY-THREE

Monday wasn't a good day.

After his miserable weekend, Arthur was in no mood for school. He drew circles on his notebook during most of his classes. By the time he got to lunch, he'd filled the entire front and back covers of his math notebook with aimless spirals.

"What's wrong?" Squeak asked, giving Arthur a sideways look as he sat down next to him.

"Nothing," Arthur snapped.

He could see Squeak's eyes blink nervously behind his old-man glasses, but he had to give the kid credit—he didn't move away.

"Okay. Just wondering."

Silently, Squeak opened his brown lunch bag and got out his usual collection of foil-wrapped items. After unwrapping each one, he slid the foil squares toward Arthur, who didn't bother to pick them up. They stayed where Squeak left them. A lonely raft of foil in the middle of the cafeteria table.

Squeak nibbled on a corner of his sandwich and eyed Arthur. "Not eating?"

"Not hungry."

"Okay . . ." Squeak paused. "If you get hungry, you can have some of my lunch if you want it."

"No thanks."

As the silence continued, Arthur became aware of something hitting him in the back. At first he thought maybe he was imagining things. It was just a light tap, and when he looked over his shoulder, nobody was there.

Then he saw the piece of hot dog hit Squeak's back.

Squeak was wearing one of his usual tucked-in shirts with a sweater vest. The piece of hot dog had mustard on it. A splat of yellowish brown was smeared on the back of Squeak's light blue vest.

Another piece of hot dog hit Arthur's neck and ricocheted onto the table.

This wasn't the first time they'd been targets in the junior high cafeteria. Getting shoved in the food line or being called Convict or Juvie Boy was about the worst it got for Arthur. Most seventh graders at Byrd still seemed to fear him a little bit. But Squeak got picked on nearly every day.

Arthur sucked in his breath, feeling his fury boiling over. "That's it," he said. He grabbed the hot dog piece off the table and started to stand up.

"Wait." Squeak put his hand on Arthur's arm to stop him. "Give me your notebook and a pen."

"What for?" Arthur turned his anger on Squeak. "Just let me handle it."

But Squeak reached out and snatched the notebook that was sitting on top of Arthur's pile of books. Picking up a pen, he began writing something in large letters. Arthur couldn't see what it was. Squeak kept his arm over the page.

It only took him a minute to finish his message, and then Arthur was shocked to see Squeak get up, put one knee on the shiny table, and scramble awkwardly onto it.

Then he stood up.

"For crying out loud, Squeak. What are you doing?" Arthur called out.

The noise in the large cafeteria gradually diminished as more and more kids noticed Squeak standing on the table in his blue vest, belted pants, and polished leather shoes. There was a lot of nervous laughter and "What's he holding?" A couple of the gym teachers who supervised the cafeteria moved closer.

Arthur couldn't see the sign. Not from where he was sitting.

"What the heck did you write?" he asked.

"I'll tell you later," Squeak answered without moving. "Just finish your lunch."

"I don't have a lunch," Arthur shot back. "Get down, Squeak, and stop acting like a moron."

"I'm not sitting down until they stop throwing things at us."

"They've stopped."

"Well, then, it's working," Squeak replied, still not budging. He held the notebook in front of him like a ridiculous shield.

Vice, the dry cornstalk of an administrator, came strolling slowly toward their corner of the cafeteria. There was a collective cheer from the students, who expected to see Squeak hauled off the table and led away. (Arthur assumed Vice was walking slowly in the hopes that Squeak would jump off the table on his own.)

Squeak didn't get the message.

"What are you holding, Reginald?" Vice said when he reached them. He squinted upward. It was probably the only time in Squeak's life he'd had someone looking up at him, Arthur couldn't help thinking. He tried not to smile.

"A sign," Squeak answered calmly.

"And what does the sign say, Reginald?" Vice asked slowly, although Arthur knew he could probably read it himself.

"It says *Go Ahead. Throw Things at Me*," Squeak answered without looking down at the notebook that he still held in front of his puny chest.

Go Ahead. Throw Things at Me.

Arthur felt a small glow of appreciation flicker inside him. He couldn't remember the last time someone had done something nice for him at school. Not since way before his dad died. And here was Squeak standing up on a table for him. Trying to protect him. Wimpy, short little Squeak was standing up for Arthur Owens, a brick-throwing delinquent. You had to admire the kid.

"You know we don't stand on tables and hold up signs in this school." Vice kept talking quietly, as if he were a bottomless well of patience.

Arthur was sure if it had been him standing on the table instead of Squeak, Vice would have called the police and had the table surrounded by cops, guns drawn.

Squeak's glasses flashed in the artificial lights as he looked down stubbornly. "It's a free country. I have the right to free speech."

"Not on a table in my cafeteria you don't."

"Doesn't say that in the Bill of Rights."

"It says it in my Bill of Rights," Vice replied, still weirdly calm.

With Vice and Squeak playing it so cool, Arthur could tell the cafeteria crowd was getting restless. Eventually, the people at the tables around them seemed to give up waiting for something to happen and went back to whatever they were doing before. The lunch noise returned to its previous level.

Vice kept staring up at Squeak with his arms crossed. Squeak kept standing. Arthur kept trying to pretend he was invisible.

"You can eat my lunch if you want to, Arthur," Squeak said after another long minute or two had passed. "I don't want it."

Arthur shook his head. "That's okay."

Vice gave Arthur a suspicious look. "Did you put him up to this cute little trick, Mr. Owens?" he said, eyes narrowing.

Before Arthur could get a word out, Squeak's voice answered indignantly from above. "He. Did. Not."

Arthur was relieved when the bell finally rang. Afterward, someone called for Vice over the loudspeaker, so he had to hurry away before he could give them a stern lecture. Squeak scrambled down from the tabletop and politely handed Arthur's notebook back to him.

"Here."

"Thanks," Arthur said hesitantly. "For doing that."

"You helped me last time. This time, it was my turn." Squeak puffed up his shoulders proudly and gave one of his goofy, too-wide grins. "I looked pretty tough up there, didn't I?"

Arthur nodded. He didn't have the heart to tell Squeak that it would probably end badly. No doubt they'd get bombarded with even more hot dogs tomorrow.

But he did let him know about the mustard.

"They got stuff on your sweater," Arthur said. "You can't walk around the halls with mustard all over your back. Here, I'll help you get it off." He spit on a napkin and dabbed at the glob between Squeak's shoulder blades. It didn't make it disappear completely, but he got the worst of it off.

THIRTY-FOUR

Arthur waited another couple of days to tell Squeak what had happened with Mr. Hampton over the weekend. He wasn't sure he trusted himself to talk about it without losing his cool.

But the scene with Officer Billie in the restaurant kept bothering him. He felt guilty for what he'd said. Mr. Hampton was dying of cancer, and he'd acted like a complete jerk. He didn't know how to undo what he'd done.

He kept picturing the garage full of gold-and-silver furniture that was supposed to be heaven. And all of those shimmering wings.

"If I tell you something that's bugging me, can you keep your mouth shut about it?" he asked Squeak while they were finishing lunch on Wednesday.

"What?" Squeak glanced up from his book, looking lost. He was studying for a big algebra test that afternoon.

Arthur sighed, already beginning to regret his decision. "Just listen to me for a minute, okay?"

"Sure. Yes." Squeak closed his textbook reluctantly.

Taking a deep breath, Arthur told Squeak the whole crazy story. How he'd found Mr. Hampton crumpled on the floor of the garage and how he'd gone to the hospital with him. How they'd talked for the first time and how he'd finally learned what the guy was doing.

"So what is it?" Squeak asked.

"Heaven," Arthur said. "He's building a sculpture of heaven."

"What?" Squeak's mouth dropped open. "Heaven?"

Without stopping to explain, Arthur pushed on with the rest of his story, telling Squeak what he'd learned from Officer Billie. How Mr. Hampton had cancer and how it was possible he might be dying.

When Arthur finished talking, Squeak's eyes were wide and unblinking behind his glasses. "Gosh, that's a lot . . . to have happen all at once," he said.

Arthur paused and swallowed, trying to keep his voice steady. "The thing is, he asked me to keep working on the project while he's in the hospital. He gave me the keys to his garage. But I don't think I can do it."

"Why not?"

Arthur picked up one of the foil squares from the table and crumpled it in his hands. He didn't like talking about his feelings, especially not about his dad.

"Because I can't deal with it again, not after my dad's death and all that stuff," he said finally. "I don't care who it is—I don't want to deal with it."

He kept on crumpling more and more foil without saying anything else. When he finished, he had a small pile of foil gumballs in front of him.

After a long silence, Squeak said, "Well, do you want my opinion?"

"I guess."

"I don't think you can give up on Mr. Hampton."

"Why not?" Arthur snapped, sounding more irritated than he meant to.

Squeak took off his glasses and wiped them carefully on his shirt. "Well, it's your probation sentence, that's one reason."

"Officer Billie said they'd find something else for me to do."

"It might be worse."

"Than working for a dying person?"

"Who knows?" Squeak shrugged. "You don't know for sure what's going to happen. Maybe the project will somehow save him. The mind is a powerful thing. Maybe building heaven . . . working on this masterpiece . . . is what's keeping him alive."

"That's crazy," Arthur replied, although he couldn't help remembering what Mr. Hampton had said in the hospital about the brick saving him. "And now you've made me feel guilty," he added. "Like if I don't help him, he might die."

"I could come along with you this Saturday and help out, if you want," Squeak offered. "Except for my violin lesson, I don't have anything else to do."

Arthur stared incredulously at Squeak. "You take *violin* lessons?"

"They only last an hour." Squeak looked embarrassed. "I'd like to see the project. Maybe if I saw it, I could give you some ideas about what to do next."

"I don't need any help," Arthur insisted, annoyed with himself for sharing too much with Squeak. There was no way someone whose biggest worry was *violin lessons* could possibly understand all the things he had to deal with in his life.

Squeak stood up and slid one knee onto the tabletop. "If you don't let me come this Saturday, I will stand up here again. I swear I will."

Arthur grabbed Squeak's elbow, accidentally knocking his pile of books to the floor. "Don't be an idiot."

Squeak's eyes were fierce behind his glasses. "Then let me come along."

"Fine," Arthur sighed. "Okay."

He was tired of fighting with everyone.

THIRTY-FIVE

Fortunately, Saturday turned out to be a decent day—a little windy, but pretty warm for the middle of February. Arthur was pleased to see it would be good weather for pushing the cart around Seventh Street collecting stuff with Squeak. Even though he hadn't called Officer Billie to tell her he wasn't quitting, he hoped the hours would still count toward his probation. He'd give Squeak the job of finding a *mirror,* he thought with a smile.

Of course, Squeak showed up for trash picking dressed as if he were about to enroll in college. Loafers. Neatly cuffed denim jeans. And a gosh-awful, bright red pullover.

"For crying out loud, what the heck are you wearing?" Arthur said when he opened the door and saw him. "Didn't I tell you to wear crummy clothes? Did you forget or what?"

"These are old," Squeak insisted.

With a loud sigh, Arthur pulled on his old elementary

school coat and yanked his black knit cap over his head. If Squeak wanted to look like an idiot collecting trash, it wasn't his problem, he tried to tell himself. He was just glad his mom and sister had left to run a few errands, so he wouldn't get the endless questions about who his new friend was, and comments about how nice it was he'd made a friend, and blah blah blah.

They started down the street, with Arthur still feeling annoyed.

"You do this every Saturday? In the snow and everything?" Squeak said after they'd only gone a few blocks. He seemed genuinely impressed.

"Yeah." Arthur shrugged. "It's not all that bad, really."

"How many more hours of probation do you have left?"

Arthur had to admit he'd lost track. "Around eighty or ninety hours, I think, but I'm not sure."

"Wow," Squeak said, shaking his head.

Arthur didn't know if he meant "wow" good or "wow" bad.

As they got closer to the neighborhood where Hampton's garage was, Arthur could see Squeak was getting more nervous. He kept taking quick looks over his shoulder. His hands were jammed in his pockets. He walked faster.

"I told you to wear old clothes," Arthur reminded him.

He knew Seventh Street wasn't the best-looking area, but it wasn't dangerous—at least, he'd never had any trouble. There was a big BEWARE OF DOG sign on a house where he had never seen any dogs. Another dilapidated house had a tabby cat that always sat in the front window. It had taken Arthur a couple of Saturdays to decide whether the cat was real. He pointed it out to Squeak.

"Really, it's a lot safer around here than in the cafeteria at Byrd," Arthur said. "Nobody is going to nail you in the back with a hot dog here."

Squeak laughed. "Okay."

As they turned at Groovy Jim's and started down the short gravel alley, Arthur gestured toward the shop. "Groovy Jim is pretty cool. I'll introduce you later."

Squeak glanced back at the shop. "Yeah, someday I'm going to get one."

"What? You want to get a tattoo?"

Squeak nodded. "Yeah. Something dangerous. Like a big white skull. Or a snake. You know, right here on my arm."

He seemed serious, so Arthur kept a straight face and tried not to laugh. He couldn't picture Squeak with a skull on his skinny white biceps. Ever.

When they got to the garage, there was no grocery cart sitting outside, of course. The place appeared as deserted as always.

"This is it?" Squeak asked, looking doubtful.

"Yeah, this is it. Nothing fancy."

Arthur could still see the tire tracks of the ambulance that had taken Mr. Hampton away. It seemed like it had been months ago instead of only a week. Shaking his head, he reached into his pocket for the keys Mr. Hampton had given to him. He hoped the guy was doing better. He hoped it wasn't a mistake that he'd brought Squeak to see his strange masterpiece. Without even thinking, he unlocked the door and pushed it open.

And there was James Hampton working inside.

THIRTY-SIX

"Whoa!" Arthur shouted, just about knocking Squeak flat to the ground behind him as he lurched backward in surprise.

The old man was sitting in one of those rolling office-type chairs in the middle of the garage, with boxes scattered around his feet. Bright bits of foil covered his lap.

"Saint Arthur, come in!" Mr. Hampton turned his chair and gestured to them, smiling a little. "I wasn't expecting you today. I was informed that you were quitting."

And I was told you were dying, Arthur thought as he stood there stupidly staring at the guy, who looked very much alive. Maybe a little thinner. But mostly okay, compared with the last time he'd seen him, in the hospital bed.

Mr. Hampton was wearing ordinary clothes. A baggy brown cardigan with a few holes in the sleeves sagged around his shoulders. He had on corduroy pants and scuffed shoes. Somewhere he'd found another pair of glasses to replace the broken ones. Behind the round black frames, the old man's eyes looked sharp and clear.

"He changed his mind about quitting," Squeak piped up behind Arthur.

Mr. Hampton's gaze shifted from Arthur to Squeak. "I see you've brought reinforcements."

"This is Squeak," Arthur mumbled, stepping aside to let Squeak come in.

"That's your friend's name? Squeak?"

Just by the tone of Mr. Hampton's voice, Arthur could tell he didn't approve of the nickname.

"It's Reginald, actually. I'm Reginald Buckley Pierce, sir." Squeak walked over to Mr. Hampton and stuck out his hand politely. "It's a pleasure to meet you."

Good grief, Arthur thought. Squeak didn't need to recite his entire birth certificate for the guy.

"Very nice to meet you, Reginald." Mr. Hampton shook Squeak's hand. Then he leaned back in his chair and folded his hands neatly in his lap. He reminded Arthur of the dignified Mr. Hampton from court again—only without the sling like the letter *A* across his chest.

"Well, boys, I wasn't expecting company today, but I sure could use the help." He shook his head. "I lost a lot of time this week. Way too much time. I had all sorts of big plans, and none of them happened, did they?"

Arthur decided not to point out to Mr. Hampton that his plans hadn't worked out because he'd almost died in his garage.

The old man waved one hand toward the shimmering

work of art. "As you can see, my vision of heaven is far from complete."

This was the first time Squeak and Arthur allowed their attention to turn toward the spectacular creation that filled the rest of the garage.

Arthur heard Squeak whisper, "Wow."

As Arthur gazed at the startling objects again—dozens upon dozens of glittering pieces crowded together—he could feel his heart fluttering just like it had when he'd first seen them. It reminded him of the feeling you got when you looked down from a tall building. How everything below looked real and unreal. That was how the creation made him feel—as if he was looking at something both real and unreal at the same time.

Now he could see how some of the pieces were made of the things he'd collected, just as Mr. Hampton had said. He recognized the red-and-gold throne chair he'd brought back from the big Victorian house, and a few of the small tables he'd found over the past two months. He was pretty sure the silver globes decorating many of the objects were lightbulbs covered in foil. And nearly every square inch of everything else was covered in foil too.

Squeak spoke up. "Arthur told me you're building heaven."

"Yes," Mr. Hampton replied. "Actually, it's the Throne of the Third Heaven. What do you think?"

"I'm not sure." Squeak looked as if he couldn't quite believe his eyes.

"Well, let me show you how it all started." Mr. Hampton

rolled his chair closer to the radiant display. He pointed out a small box covered with layers of metallic decorations near their feet. It resembled a fancy jewelry box.

"There, pick that one up," he said to Arthur.

"You pick it up, Squeak," Arthur insisted. The box looked like it would fall apart if you breathed on it.

"Are you sure?" Squeak glanced uncertainly at Mr. Hampton. Arthur could tell he didn't want to pick it up either.

"Hand it to me," Mr. Hampton commanded.

Acting like he was lifting a tray of eggs, Squeak slowly picked up the box and handed it to Mr. Hampton.

"This was my first piece," the old man said.

There was a little handwritten tag on it, Arthur noticed, in some strange language.

"I made it on Guam after I had my first vision." Mr. Hampton looked sharply from Squeak to Arthur. "Now, which one of you knows where Guam is and why it's important?"

Arthur was extremely relieved when Squeak jumped in to answer that it was an island in the Pacific where the Allies had fought the Japanese in World War II.

Right then and there, Arthur decided that if he ever got on a TV quiz show, he'd definitely want Squeak on his side.

"Very good, young man. He's a smart kid, isn't he? Keep him around," Mr. Hampton said to Arthur. Then his face grew serious. "I served on Guam in the Second World War, and when we got there, it was a terrible place. Everything was in pieces. Everywhere you looked there were pieces—of bombs, of planes, of people."

As he spoke, Hampton's voice shook and the box trembled dangerously in his hands. Arthur thought they probably shouldn't be talking about war and upsetting the guy. Especially since he'd just gotten out of the hospital. He glanced toward Squeak, trying to send him a subliminal message to change the subject.

"Every night, I had dreams, terrible dreams, about the things I saw," Hampton continued.

Arthur's mind went back to his own bad dreams: The bottles rolling away. The cops coming to their door. Trying to save his father and never succeeding.

"And then one night," Mr. Hampton said, "I'd had enough. I couldn't stand the war any longer. I wanted to die and be done with it. And that's the night when I had my first vision, my first dream, of building heaven out of broken things."

He held up the fragile box for them to look at again. Now Arthur could see the bits of wood and glass and metal he'd used. Tiny nails and pins held the parts together. One piece of metal had numbers stamped on it. Another looked like a round silver button. There was a rusted hinge from something and a metal handle or knob from something else.

"I made this box from the broken things I found on Guam. This is Death and War turned into something beautiful."

It *was* beautiful. Arthur could hear himself gulp in the silence that followed. He swore he could hear Squeak's eyelids blinking really fast behind his glasses too.

Neither of them knew what to say. The usual things they might have said—*cool, wow, that's great, that's crazy, nobody would guess that*—seemed completely wrong. So they just stood there blinking and swallowing loudly.

Finally, Squeak blurted out, "Why do you call it the Throne of the Third Heaven?"

"Don't know." Hampton shrugged his thin shoulders. He passed the small box back to Squeak, who set it gently on the floor. "It was the number I saw in my dream. A big number three in the sky." He drew the number in the air with his hand. "I never question what I'm told. Some things in this world are meant to remain a mystery."

Mr. Hampton began rolling his office chair toward the far side of the garage with his feet. "Enough talking for now, boys. We've got a lot of work to do."

THE THIRD IMPORTANT THING

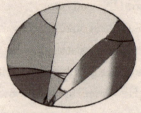

It is not easy to wrap a lightbulb with tiny scraps of foil.

Arthur discovered this pretty quickly.

Mr. Hampton needed ten lightbulbs to decorate the top of a silver pedestal he was making for the collection. The pedestal would go to the left of the red chair—the throne—to balance a pedestal on the right. Everything in heaven was perfectly balanced, he said.

Mr. Hampton used foil-wrapped bulbs to decorate a lot of his pieces. "Lights in the darkness," he called them.

After making his first one, Arthur called them a big pain in the butt.

First you had to put rubber cement on the lightbulb. Not too much or it would drip all over the place, Hampton warned. Not too little or the foil would slide off. Then, with one hand carefully holding the sticky bulb, you had to grab a tiny square of tinfoil and press it firmly to the side.

Without. Breaking. The bulb.

This was the part of the process that made Arthur very nervous. The bulbs were glass, of course. Ridiculously thin glass. Arthur's hands weren't very careful. He didn't trust himself not to crush, pulverize, or drop a bulb.

Squeak had much more patience. And smaller hands.

So Arthur would brush rubber cement onto the bulb and hand the foil scraps to Squeak, who would press them gently around the glass globe, as if he was working with an unexploded bomb.

Surprisingly, Arthur could still recognize where a lot of the foil scraps had come from. He could pick out the ones that were Squeak's lunch foil, the tops of TV dinner trays, Christmas gift paper, and wine bottle wrappers.

Arthur remembered how people in the neighborhood always used to call the Junk Man a crazy old drunk when they saw him sticking empty wine and liquor bottles in his coat pockets. It made Arthur feel guilty to think about it now. Nobody would have guessed he was using them for their foil wrappers.

"Best foil you can get, hands down," Mr. Hampton told Arthur and Squeak when he showed them how to wrap the bulbs. "The other stuff works fine, but the bottle foil has the most shimmer."

He liked to use a lot of different layers on each bulb. "More layers equals more shine."

Arthur wasn't sure he believed this theory, but Squeak was the kind of person who followed directions 100 percent.

He insisted on wrapping every bulb in about a half-dozen layers. Every shiny corner had to be glued down and pressed perfectly smooth against the bulb. He wouldn't go on to the next one until Mr. Hampton inspected it and gave his approval.

Arthur was glad when they finally finished the bulbs and could move on to something else. Their next job was much more suited to him. They had to smash a bunch of mirrors into tiny pieces.

Now it was Squeak's turn to be nervous.

They were supposed to put the mirrors in paper grocery bags and smash them with a hammer. That was the safest way to break them, according to Mr. Hampton. Once the mirrors were broken up, they poured the fragments into a box for him to use later as decoration on the wings.

"Gives the angel wings their sparkle," he said.

But Squeak was convinced that if they broke the mirrors, they'd be causing themselves years of bad luck. "I don't think this is a good idea," he whispered to Arthur. "You're not supposed to break mirrors. It's really bad luck in a lot of cultures. Haven't you ever heard of a broken mirror bringing you seven years of bad luck? I don't think we should be doing this."

Arthur shrugged. "I don't care. I've already had a ton of bad luck. I'm not afraid of a stupid mirror." He picked up the hammer, feeling strangely invincible. "Maybe it'll have the opposite effect for me." He laughed. "Who knows . . . maybe smashing a mirror will bring me good luck."

And then, after Squeak moved a safe distance away from the potential bad luck *and* closed his eyes, Arthur broke his first mirror.

It felt good.

Great, actually.

"Hand me another one," he said to Squeak, who looked reluctant to touch anything resembling a mirror. So Arthur picked out one by himself from the stack leaning against the wall of the garage and put it in a paper bag. Lifting his hammer, he shattered another one. It reminded him of his earth science class—of the continental plates cracking apart. Only he was the one shattering the plates.

"Fourteen," Squeak said faintly.

"What?" Arthur looked up.

"Fourteen years of bad luck. Seven times two."

"I've already had that much bad luck in one year," Arthur said, feeling happier than he had in a long time. "I'm going to break another one." And he did.

"Twenty-one," he and Squeak said together.

Arthur broke three more mirrors before Hampton looked up from attaching a large pair of foil-wrapped angel wings to one of the pedestals. "Okay, that's enough, boys. That's plenty of mirrors. You can stop now."

"Good," Squeak whispered, seeming relieved.

Arthur wished he could have broken a few more. As he carried the forty-two years' worth of bad luck—or good luck, depending on your perspective—over to Mr. Hampton, he felt as if he'd been set free of something, as if some big shadow over his life had been taken away.

After his dad's accident, he'd spent months worrying about what might happen next. He'd worried about his mom and Barbara all the time. Then, after he threw the brick, he started worrying about who he was—whether he was a bad kid who'd end up in trouble just like his dad. It was a big mirror of bad luck hanging over his head every day.

And now he had smashed that mirror into a million shiny pieces.

This was the third important thing.

THIRTY-SEVEN

When Monday arrived, Arthur decided he'd better call Officer Billie at work, just to let her know the guards at juvie didn't need to get the bunk above Slash ready for him. He wasn't quitting yet.

As usual, Officer Billie answered on the first ring.

"It's Arthur Owens," Arthur said.

"So, you aren't quitting," Officer Billie guessed even before Arthur could tell her.

"How did you—"

"I told you, I've been doing this for years. I know everything. Nothing surprises me. I knew you weren't going to quit even before you knew you weren't going to quit."

"All right," Arthur said, getting annoyed by her again. "Just wanted to let you know."

And then a small idea—okay, a kind of devious one—occurred to him.

"So—I was wondering, do you know what the seven most important things in the world are?" he asked, trying to make the question sound innocent.

"What?"

"The seven most important things . . . do you know what they are?" Arthur repeated.

"Is this a question for school, Mr. Owens?" Officer Billie sounded irritated. "Because I don't do homework. If you need to know the answer to something for class, look it up yourself. The most important thing to me is seeing that you don't mess up, got it?"

"Yes," Arthur replied politely. "Thanks."

Smiling to himself, he hung up the phone. So Officer Billie didn't know everything, he realized. She didn't know about Mr. Hampton's Throne.

THIRTY-EIGHT

It turned out that Arthur wasn't the only one keeping secrets from people. The next day, his sister dropped a bombshell about their mom.

"Mom's got a boyfriend who's coming over for supper on Friday," she told Arthur while they were sitting in the kitchen polishing off a bag of corn chips after school.

"What?" Arthur felt as if someone had suddenly dumped a barrel of ice water over his head. His whole body turned cold in an instant.

"But I'm not supposed to tell you," Barbara replied quickly as she shoved a handful of Fritos into her mouth. "Mom said she's going to talk to you about it later. When the time is right."

Arthur sat frozen in his dad's chair in the banana-yellow kitchen that his dad had painted, unable to believe what his sister had just said. His mom had a *boyfriend*? And he was *coming over to their house for supper*?

This was way worse than throwing out his dad's stuff. This was throwing out his dad and replacing him with someone else. *How could his mom do this to him? To them?*

Barbara stopped eating and stared at him. "You look kind of strange. Are you okay, Arthur? You look like you're going to throw up."

Arthur shook his head. "I'm fine."

She pushed the Fritos bag closer to him. "You can have the rest if you want."

"That's okay."

"You want to watch some cartoons with me?"

"No."

Barbara tilted her blond head, studying him. "I think you look sick. You should go to bed. I can bring you a thermometer and a bucket if you want one."

"Stop it. Just go and watch some TV, Barbara," Arthur snapped.

"All right." Barbara slid off the chair. She bounced from one foot to the other, standing in the kitchen doorway as if she was uncertain about leaving. Or needed to pee.

"You sure?" she said.

Arthur had to bite his tongue to keep himself from shouting *SHUT UP AND LEAVE ME ALONE!* at Barbara. Instead, he looked at the clock above the stove and told her in the most patient voice he could manage that if she didn't hurry, she was going to miss *Looney Tunes*.

"Okay, I'm going." But before she left, Barbara said in a rush, "His name is Roger and I've met him already and he's pretty nice. He's a carpenter. Do you know what they do?"

Arthur felt his heart squeezing into a tighter and tighter ball. It was just a coincidence, he tried to tell himself.

"He builds things out of pieces of wood!" Barbara shouted proudly. "And he's making a birdhouse for Mom, but don't tell her, okay?"

"Okay." Arthur nodded, feeling numb.

There was no way some loser named Roger could be the fourth most important thing.

THE FOURTH IMPORTANT THING

Roger the Carpenter wasn't the kind of person Arthur expected him to be. He'd pictured a slimeball guy who had probably swept his mom off her feet because she was lonely and sad and needed someone to talk to.

Arthur's mom told him they'd met at her new job—the dentist's office job that she'd only had since the beginning of January. Roger had been building some new cabinets for the dentist, and they'd chatted over lunch.

"All he brought to eat was a candy bar, so I gave him some of my homemade ham salad," she said. Then he'd asked her out for coffee after work. And they'd gone out for coffee a few times since then.

"He's been very nice to me," Arthur's mom insisted. "So I invited him to supper on Friday. Will you at least meet him and see what you think?"

He promised nothing.

• • •

Roger arrived early on Friday. Arthur heard the doorbell ring at five, but he didn't wander downstairs to meet the guy until Roger had already been there for about half an hour, talking with his mom and Barbara.

As it turned out, Roger was balding and short and looked about ten years older than Arthur's dad had been. He wore a striped shirt tucked into pants that appeared to have been bought that afternoon. The only thing missing was the price tag.

"You must be Arthur," the guy said, standing up quickly when Arthur came into the living room. He nearly knocked over his drink on the shaky tray table beside the chair. "I'm Roger Dent. Good to meet you."

Roger *Dent* from the *dentist's* office. Good grief. It was like being in a bad TV comedy.

"Barbara, go and get the lovely birdhouse Roger made for us so your brother can see it," Arthur's mom said in this strangely happy voice that sounded exactly like Wilma Flintstone's.

Barbara carried the birdhouse from the hallway and set it in Arthur's lap. "What do you think?" she said, hands on her hips.

Arthur had to admit it looked as if Roger Dent had put some serious time into it. The roof had tiny shingles made of the ends of Popsicle sticks. There were two small windows on the front outlined with matchsticks.

"Isn't it beautiful?" Arthur's mom raved.

From the starstruck look on his mom's face, Arthur had no doubt Roger the Carpenter, who made beautiful things out of wood, was the fourth most important thing. At least for his mom.

"Are we ready to eat now?" Arthur's mom asked everyone in the same Wilma Flintstone voice.

Arthur really wanted to say no, but he didn't want to upset his mom.

Supper seemed to last forever.

Unlike Arthur's dad, Roger Dent was not a big talker. So there were long silences when all you could hear was food being chewed and silverware clinking on the plates. Between the silences, Barbara told endless stories about her school friends: who was mad at who, who was friends with who. And Arthur's mom kept nervously asking if everything tasted okay and if anybody needed more food.

Arthur tried not to glance in Roger Dent's direction at all. At least the guy wasn't sitting in his dad's old seat. Arthur had told his mom he wouldn't be part of the dinner with Roger—or any dinner, ever—if her boyfriend sat in his dad's chair.

So his mom was sitting there instead.

He wondered what his mom had told Roger Dent about them—if the guy knew about his dad dying in a motorcycle accident and about him being in juvie. It probably wasn't the kind of news you shared until you knew somebody pretty well, he decided. *Yeah, my husband only died a few months ago and my son is a brick-throwing juvenile delinquent* probably wasn't a good conversation starter.

Toward the end of the meal, Arthur's mom looked over at him and said in this shaky-tense sort of voice, "You've been quiet, Arthur."

Arthur didn't dare point out that Roger Dent hadn't exactly been a great conversationalist either. He could see that his mom was on the verge of losing it. And he knew he'd better not push her much closer to the edge.

"So, um, other than birdhouses, what kinds of stuff do you build?" he asked Roger Dent, trying to sound slightly interested.

Which he wasn't, of course.

But the guy grabbed hold of that question and wouldn't let go.

He talked for about thirty minutes straight, reciting all of the projects he'd done—kitchen cabinets, bookshelves, garden sheds, playhouses, even a custom doghouse for some movie star's dog once.

Roger said he'd learned carpentry from his grandfather. Then he went into a long story about how he'd started his own business with nothing but a box of tools from his grandpa and a rusted-out Ford truck. "Until I got my first job, I lived in that truck," he told them. He described how he'd slept in parking lots and stayed at campgrounds.

The story was more interesting than Arthur had thought

it would be. Although he wouldn't admit this to anyone, there were times he'd thought it would be fun to build houses someday. He remembered designing a house for an art class project, back in the sixth grade.

He'd drawn it with a third-floor "tower" all for himself. The tower had its own bedroom, living room, and bathroom. Plus, there was a swimming pool on the roof and a helicopter landing pad in the front yard. (Okay, that was a little crazy—but hey, he'd gotten an A-plus.)

By the time Roger finished talking, the rest of the food was cold. But Arthur could tell his mom and Roger Dent were a lot happier. His mom had this goofy smile on her face.

Arthur wasn't sure how he felt. Loyal and disloyal to his dad at the same time. Mostly, he wished he'd just kept his big mouth shut. It was a lot easier to dislike someone you didn't know anything about.

THIRTY-NINE

One of Arthur's favorite memories of his dad was the time they made a Pinewood Derby car for Cub Scouts when Arthur was eight or nine years old.

By itself, Cub Scouts was not one of his favorite memories. He had missed a lot of meetings because his dad would go out with his buddies and forget about them. Or he'd come home smelling like beer and cigarettes and Arthur would suddenly get a stomachache and not want to go to the meeting. Especially after one of the kids said once, "Your dad always smells kind of weird, doesn't he?"

But making the Pinewood Derby car was something Arthur would never forget.

Most kids didn't have the advantage of having a mechanic for a dad. He remembered how they worked on the project for a couple of weekends. Designing the shape. Cutting the body from a smooth block of white pine. Painting the car with real auto body paint. His car was neon blue with white racing stripes.

It won second place. Arthur still had the red ribbon hanging up in his closet. They'd gone out to celebrate, which was the only time Arthur had eaten a steak dinner in a restaurant in his life.

He wasn't sure why helping Mr. Hampton make angel wings the next Saturday reminded him of building the Pinewood Derby car with his dad, but it did.

Squeak couldn't come along—a violin concert, he said—so it was just Arthur and Mr. Hampton working in the garage.

"We're short on wings," he said when Arthur walked in. "You can help me with wings today."

Arthur was surprised to see that Mr. Hampton looked pretty good again. He wondered if maybe Officer Billie had been mistaken about the cancer. He couldn't see anything wrong with the guy, other than the fact that he was wearing the same holey brown cardigan sweater as the last Saturday and he didn't get up from his rolling chair when Arthur walked in—just used his feet to turn himself partway around.

"You can work over there at the table." Mr. Hampton pointed to one of the rickety sawhorse tables in a far corner of the garage. "I need you to draw two sets of angel wings about, oh"—he glanced toward his creation, as if trying to visualize where they'd go—"about thirty-six inches across."

Arthur had no idea how to draw angel wings.

"Do you have something I could copy from?" he asked Mr. Hampton, who was starting to glue a row of foil decorations along the edge of a table.

"What?" He turned.

"Do you have any pictures of angel wings I could trace or copy?" Arthur repeated.

"Just use what you've seen." Mr. Hampton went back to his work.

Arthur wasn't sure what the guy meant. Did he really think he'd *seen* real angel wings?

"Uh, do you mean real ones?" Arthur said. "Or ones in, uh, books and stuff?"

"Oh, for goodness' sake!" The old man glared at Arthur as he got up from his chair. "I'll do them myself."

Arthur noticed that Mr. Hampton moved slowly as he came toward the worktable, but maybe he had always walked that way. It was hard not to notice every little thing now and worry that it might be a sign of something being wrong.

After pausing to catch his breath for a minute, Mr. Hampton took the pencil from Arthur's hand. "Here, I'll draw one. Angel wings are like bird wings, right?"

"Sure." Arthur nodded.

Mr. Hampton glanced at him oddly. "Of course they are. Only larger, depending on the angel. Two wings per angel. No two are the same. Every pattern is different. Colors and iridescence are different. Some angels are like peacocks. Others are less flashy. Like city pigeons."

Arthur had never pictured angels as city pigeons.

"Watch. You draw them like this." His hands trembling ever so slightly, Mr. Hampton began sketching a pair of wings on a large piece of cardboard. Arthur noticed it was a flattened grocery carton. Probably one he had collected.

When he was done, he handed the design to Arthur. "There. Now you cut them out."

After Arthur cut out the wings, the rough cardboard edges had to be sanded smooth. Then the wings were covered in gold or silver foil. Hampton wanted each wing to be made of four or five layers of foil-wrapped cardboard. He liked to alternate gold and silver layers—with a little purple paper sometimes—so the wings looked sort of three-dimensional when they were finished.

Arthur spent most of his four hours working on only one wing.

"Anything of value takes time," Hampton declared.

As they worked, Arthur kept thinking about his dad and the Pinewood Derby car. Maybe it was the smell of the glue making him delirious, but if he closed his eyes, he could almost picture being in their garage at home, with his dad standing beside him as they sanded and painted the race car.

"I used to work on stuff with my dad," he heard himself saying to Hampton, and then instantly regretted it. Mr. Hampton didn't know his dad. Or care, probably. Plus, talking about his dad always made his voice do embarrassing things.

"Did you?" Hampton didn't look up from the wing he was gluing and wrapping. "Tell me more about him."

Arthur studied Hampton's face. Was he just saying that to be polite? Or did he really want to know?

Arthur couldn't decide.

He figured Mr. Hampton might like hearing the story about the Pinewood Derby car, since it made his dad sound like an average guy who built cars with his kid. But the whole time he was talking about making the car—the special paint they used, how they tested it, and how they came in second to a kid who had won three years in a row with the same car—Mr. Hampton didn't look up from his work or seem interested in a thing.

When he was done, Arthur felt stupid for having babbled on so long about his dad. "Anyhow, that's one of the main things I remember about him," he finished.

"Do you still have it?" Mr. Hampton asked finally.

"Have what?"

"The car."

Arthur really hoped he didn't want it for his masterpiece. He wouldn't give up the car for anything. Not even for heaven.

"Yeah, I've got it somewhere, I think," he replied vaguely, even though he knew exactly where it was. He kept it in a box in the back of his closet with the warning *Don't Open or You'll Die* scrawled across the top. Just in case his sister got any ideas about borrowing it for her Barbies.

"Well, you should keep it. Your father sounds like he was a good man." Mr. Hampton nodded as he drew another small wing. "And he wore those angel wings on his hat. So he must have been a good man."

Arthur's eyes darted toward Mr. Hampton. He couldn't tell if the guy was serious about the wings or joking.

"The wings were for motorcycles," he tried to explain, since Mr. Hampton didn't seem to know what they were. "It's a logo. You know, Harley-Davidson. They didn't mean anything. He rode motorcycles."

"Oh yes." The old man pressed his lips together and nodded solemnly. "That's what I thought." Then he shrugged and smiled a little. "But you never know about angels, right?" He pointed at a bottle of glue near Arthur. "Hand me some glue, young man. I'm just about finished with this piece."

Arthur passed the glue to him. "Really, my dad wasn't an angel."

Mr. Hampton chuckled to himself. "None of us are."

"But he wasn't all bad," he added quickly, just in case his dad might be listening, wherever he was.

"I'm sure he wasn't. Tell me some more of the good stuff."

This was the point when Arthur definitely wished he'd never opened his big mouth. He could feel a lump already rising in his throat. He really wanted to change the subject. "There's not much else to say about him," he mumbled. "That's it."

"Food . . . what'd your dad like to eat?" the old man inquired as he put a careful line of glue around the edge of the wing he was finishing. "He a big eater or not?"

In spite of himself, Arthur smiled. "Yeah, he loved burgers and fries. And chili. He made killer chili. Every January, or whenever it got cold, he used to cook a big pot for all the guys at work. There'd be ingredients strewn all over our kitchen when he was done. My mom would have a fit. But everybody at the shop loved his chili. The hotter, the better."

"Me too." Mr. Hampton nodded. "Give me a big pot of chili with a slab of warm corn bread in the middle of winter. Nothing better than that." He pressed a piece of foil onto the glue. "What else? He play music or sing or anything?"

Arthur shook his head. "No, but he listened to the radio all the time. He liked Johnny Cash, anything by Johnny Cash. And he always watched *The Price Is Right* on Friday nights if he wasn't out with his buddies. Nobody—not even my little sister—was allowed to bug him during *The Price Is Right*. He'd throw a pillow at you if you interrupted his show."

Mr. Hampton laughed. "Yeah, I like that one too."

They kept talking about Arthur's dad for a while longer, in between gluing and wrapping more wings. They chatted about what kind of work his dad did. How he got started as a mechanic. His favorite cars. Arthur even told Mr. Hampton about his dad putting up the Christmas tree every year— how there couldn't be any dark spots or black holes. Mr. Hampton loved that story.

"Don't want any black holes in my masterpiece either," he said, nodding. "I want the whole garage filled up with gold and silver. No space left at all."

Arthur couldn't help asking, "How will you know when you're done?"

In an instant, Mr. Hampton's expression changed and he glared at Arthur. "A saint's work is never finished, young man."

"Okay, yeah. Sorry." Arthur shut up and went back to

wrapping foil around another scrap of cardboard. Sometimes he couldn't understand Mr. Hampton. One minute, he would seem perfectly normal, and then the next minute, he'd say something crazy about angel wings or being a saint and you'd wonder what the heck he was talking about.

But he was the first person in months who had asked about his dad's life instead of his death—Arthur had to give him credit for that. Almost nobody else cared that his dad had made great chili and listened to Johnny Cash and watched *The Price Is Right*. All most people wanted to know was why he'd been drinking and racing his motorcycle in the rain.

Arthur shook his head. Life was strange. Who could have guessed that the person who would be the most interested in his dad's life would be the Junk Man who had taken his stuff?

FORTY

The next week, Barbara got chicken pox and Arthur got sick with the flu that was going around, so he missed his last Saturday of probation in February. Squeak volunteered to do his hours instead, but Arthur knew Officer Billie would never agree to that, so he didn't even bother to ask.

In March, the weather was mostly gray and damp. Arthur got used to slogging around Seventh Street in the rain. When it was too miserable outside, he would help Mr. Hampton with gluing foil and making wings. One Saturday, Mr. Hampton sent him to the library to research pictures of crowns for the display. "What kinds of crowns?" he asked Mr. Hampton before he left.

"Heavenly ones, what else?" the old man said impatiently.

Arthur knew better than to ask the librarians for help with finding heavenly crowns. He looked up *crowns* in *The*

World Book Encyclopedia and did sketches of some famous ones for Mr. Hampton.

Fortunately, the month of April finally brought some sunshine and color back into the world. At first it was just a few patches here and there, but then the color spread out to cover everything else.

Squeak came to help on a couple of the Saturdays in April. One afternoon, they cut stars out of cardboard for Mr. Hampton to use as decoration on some of his pieces.

"You're a lot better at making things now," Squeak noticed as Arthur was working an eight-pointed star with little balls of foil on each point. Arthur showed him how he'd come up with designs for different stars and wings in his school notebooks.

"I do a lot of these in class," he said, holding up one of his notebooks. "I've got pages full of them."

Squeak shook his head. "You should be paying attention in class."

Arthur rolled his eyes. "Please."

When they weren't working in the garage, Squeak and Arthur took the grocery cart around the neighborhood to collect the usual stuff on Mr. Hampton's list. Arthur had a routine now. He knew where to get a lot of the things without having to search around too much.

The body shop down the street saved lightbulbs, busted car mirrors, and coffee cans for him. The small grocery store across from Groovy Jim's always had cardboard boxes and empty bottles. Foil was harder to find, but a week's worth of foil from Squeak's lunches did add up. Tossed-out furniture was plentiful on almost every curb in April.

"Spring-cleaning," Hampton told Arthur. "You'll find a lot of good stuff now."

He was right. Arthur couldn't believe what people threw away. Sometimes it was hard to focus on the Seven Most Important Things with all of the other great things people were pitching out.

On their treks through the neighborhood, Squeak and Arthur found rusty bicycles leaning against garbage cans. A cracked skateboard. A kid's red wagon with one missing wheel. A telescope with a broken stand. Old birdcages. Discarded fish tanks.

Surprisingly enough, Roger the Carpenter turned out to be useful for something after all.

He could fix things.

The skateboard—which Arthur kept for himself—had a hairline crack at one end of the board.

"No problem," Roger said when Arthur showed it to him after another Friday dinner. (The dinners had become a regular thing.) "I'll get right on it."

By the next Friday, Arthur had an almost-new skateboard.

Eventually, Squeak got a telescope with an almost-new

stand. Barbara got an almost-new wagon and bike. Arthur kept a fish tank and birdcage for himself in case he decided to get a pet someday. He'd never had a pet.

When Arthur's mom asked where everything was coming from, he told her they were helping James Hampton and his neighbors clean out their garages. "Spring-cleaning," he said. It wasn't a complete lie.

THE FIFTH IMPORTANT THING

The first Saturday in May was a perfect kind of day.

The turquoise sky reminded Arthur of the teardrop lamp he'd collected for Mr. Hampton way back in December. The warm air made it feel like the start of summer. It was the kind of day when his dad would have taken his motorcycle out for a spin, Arthur thought. (And then he wished he hadn't thought about it.)

It was so nice outside that Arthur would have liked to stay home and shoot some baskets in the driveway instead of going to work for Mr. Hampton all day.

But the end of his probation was still a long way off. If he'd done the math right, he wouldn't be done until the middle of July. (And then he wished he hadn't figured that out.)

Surprisingly, Mr. Hampton was sitting outside in his office chair when Arthur finally arrived. He had no idea how the guy had managed to roll his chair across the gravel and weeds by himself, but there he was, in a small square of sunlight outside the garage, with his eyes closed and his hands folded in his lap.

Of course, Arthur's first panicked thought was that something bad had happened to him again. He kicked the gravel in the alley as he hurried toward the guy, hoping the sound might wake him up.

Thankfully, Hampton's eyes opened as he got closer. Arthur tried not to let him see his big sigh of relief.

"Beautiful day, isn't it?" Mr. Hampton said, waving a shaky hand at the sky. "Thought you might not want to show up today because it's so nice."

"No, I'm here," Arthur replied, doing his best to hide the fact that the old man had guessed right. He pointed toward the garage. "So what are we working on today?"

"Well, first, I was hoping you'd go and buy me an orange soda over at the grocery across the street." Mr. Hampton pulled a crumpled dollar bill from his gray sweater pocket. Arthur couldn't imagine how the guy could stand to be wearing a sweater in the hot sunshine. No wonder he needed a drink. "I've got such a taste for an orange soda this morning," he said.

"Sure," Arthur answered, taking the money. "I can get that for you. Any certain kind?"

Mr. Hampton nodded. "Nesbitt's, if they have it. That's what I always used to drink. Buy one for yourself too. And don't worry about bringing me back the change," he called out as Arthur left.

Luckily, the shop across the street had plenty of bottles on ice. Arthur brought back three, letting his shirt get soaked as he carried them. It felt good.

Mr. Hampton watched him as he returned. "You got three bottles with you? Who's going to drink all that?"

"It's a warm day," Arthur said as he handed an open bottle to Mr. Hampton.

"Well, yes, I suppose you're right." Hampton nodded.

Arthur pulled another chair out of the garage, sat down, and picked up a bottle for himself. He tilted the soda back and took a big gulp. He'd never tried Nesbitt's before, but it wasn't bad. However, Mr. Hampton only took a tiny sip, he noticed.

"Something wrong with it?"

"Just enjoying it, that's all." The old man put down the bottle and closed his eyes again. Something about the scene seemed odd to Arthur. The guy was sitting in the sunshine in a heavy sweater, not looking warm at all. He'd only taken a small sip of the nice cold soda. Then he'd tucked the bottle carefully beside him in the chair.

"You feeling okay?"

"Much better now, thank you." Mr. Hampton pretended to smile—although Arthur wasn't really convinced—and then he changed the subject. "You know, I used to catch crawdads to buy soda pop when I was your age. You know what craw-dads are?"

Arthur shook his head. He was a city kid. He'd never seen a crawdad.

"Well, it doesn't matter." The old man waved one hand. "Where I grew up in the South, people used to eat them.

They were a delicacy. So I'd catch a whole bucketful of crawdads in the river and take them to the fellow who ran the market in town. He'd give me a free soda pop for every bucketful. Then he'd sell those crawdads for three times what I got. But it wasn't a bad deal." He chuckled. "Not for the time. Not for a kid."

Arthur kept looking at the old guy hunched in the office chair in front of him, trying to imagine what he might have been like as a kid. It was almost impossible. He wondered what Mr. Hampton's family had been like. Did he have any brothers and sisters? What sort of place had he grown up in?

"You polished off that bottle pretty quick, young man," Hampton said, interrupting Arthur's thoughts. He pointed to the almost-empty Nesbitt's bottle Arthur was holding.

"Yeah, I guess," Arthur agreed, wishing he hadn't finished it so fast, since he didn't think it would be polite to burp in front of Mr. Hampton.

"What you should do now is go and stick your empty bottle on that tree over there." The old man nodded in the direction of a straggly shrub next to the garage.

"What?" Arthur turned to squint at it over his shoulder.

"That's what we used to do when I was a kid," Mr. Hampton continued. "Every spring, my mother used to have each of us—my sister and my brothers and me—stick a soda bottle on a tree we had in the backyard. I don't know if it was a Southern thing or a family tradition or what. My mother always said it was a way to empty out the things we weren't proud of from the year before. Bad grades or lying or being prideful or whatever it was. You put the bottle on the end of a branch in the springtime, she used to say, and everything you'd been bottling up inside you would pour out onto the ground and disappear forever."

Mr. Hampton looked sideways at Arthur. "So what would you choose as the thing you're least proud of, Saint Arthur?"

"Throwing the brick at you," Arthur answered, without even pausing to think. He felt guilty he hadn't apologized yet. He'd started to say something a couple of times when they'd been working in the garage together, but then he'd chickened out.

"I told you that you saved the project," Mr. Hampton said.

"I still feel bad."

"Well, then go and put your soda bottle on the tree. That way all the guilt you're still carrying around inside you will flow out and be gone for good."

Arthur said he'd probably cause a flood.

"I wouldn't worry about that," Hampton replied with a wry smile. "Well, go on." He waved one arm. "And here." He dumped the rest of his soda on the ground beside his chair. "Take mine. Lord knows I've done some things I'm not proud of this past year."

Although it seemed silly, Arthur took the bottles over to the shrub and stuck them on the ends of two half-dead branches. They looked ridiculous—two empty Nesbitt's bottles wobbling on the ends of a straggly bush.

But he had to admit it kind of helped. He pictured all the anger, frustration, sadness, guilt, and everything else he couldn't deal with pouring out and hissing as it hit the ground, the way rain does on hot pavement.

"So how long do you keep the bottles on the tree?" he asked Hampton when he got back to his chair.

He laughed. "Till they run out."

Well, that was never gonna happen, Arthur decided.

He pointed at the third, unopened soda and asked Hampton, "You want the last one?"

"No, I've had plenty. You can have it, young man." Mr. Hampton tugged his sweater tighter around his shoulders, as if he was getting chilled. The square of sunlight had moved away from their spot. "And after you're done with it, you can leave it on the tree for the Throne of the Third Heaven," he added.

Arthur looked at Mr. Hampton in surprise. "Why?"

The old man sighed and squinted upward. "For all the regrets I have about it. See, I wasted too much time in life before doing what I was meant to do. That's the mistake I made. I didn't start soon enough." He pointed a shaky finger at Arthur. "Take it from me: Don't wait for a better time. I waited too long, and now the people aren't going to get to see everything I want them to see."

Arthur had no idea what Mr. Hampton was talking about. "Who won't get to see everything?"

"The people who are coming."

Arthur looked around the empty alleyway. "What people?"

"You'll see," Mr. Hampton insisted mysteriously, closing his eyes again.

There was a long silence. Arthur wasn't sure if Hampton had fallen asleep or what, but he kept quiet. The guy seemed like he needed to rest.

Mr. Hampton's eyes opened again. "If something happens to me, I want you to promise me something."

"All right," Arthur said uneasily. "What is it?"

"I want you to promise me that you'll be the next Director of Special Projects for the State of Eternity."

Arthur thought he was kidding. "I don't think you'd really want me to direct any project for you," he said with a half-joking laugh. "I'm not very good at the state of anything, let alone eternity."

"No, this is very serious. It is not a joke, young man." Mr. Hampton leaned forward, his dark eyes gazing hard at Arthur. "I want you to promise me that if something happens to me, you will be the next Director of Special Projects for the State of Eternity and save my creation"—he pointed at the garage—"for the people who are coming."

"All right." Arthur shrugged. "Sure."

"No, I want you to say you promise me."

"Okay, I promise," Arthur agreed, just so Hampton would calm down and stop talking about crazy stuff like invisible people coming down the alley and states of eternity.

"I'm counting on you, Saint Arthur," Hampton told him. He squinted up at the sky. "Now I think we'd best get busy working before it gets too late."

After putting the last bottle on the tree, they went into the garage. Arthur helped Hampton move his office chair across the gravel because he said he wasn't feeling up to it. "A little tired, is all," he said.

They spent the rest of the afternoon cutting out cardboard stars to decorate the base of a new table Mr. Hampton was putting together.

Although Arthur didn't know it, those were the last stars he'd make with him.

Three days later, James Hampton was dead.

FORTY-ONE

Officer Billie came to Arthur's house on Tuesday afternoon to tell him what had happened—that Mr. Hampton had been taken to the hospital on Monday night and despite everything they did, the doctors weren't able to save him. He had died early that morning.

The whole time Officer Billie was talking, Arthur kept thinking about what Mr. Hampton had said on Saturday. *If something happens to me . . .*

He'd never imagined those words would come true so soon. Not in a million years. Maybe Mr. Hampton had seemed more tired than usual on Saturday and had said some odd things, but they'd made a bunch of stars and Mr. Hampton had started to design a new table for his masterpiece. It wasn't possible that he was dead.

When Arthur didn't say anything, Officer Billie patted his shoulder awkwardly and said if he needed to talk about his feelings, he could call anytime. "I realize this is tough news to hear."

Even though he was afraid to ask, Arthur knew he had to find out about the garage and Mr. Hampton's project.

"He kind of put me in charge of some things in his garage," he managed to say in an almost-steady voice before the officer left. "What do you think is going to happen with everything?"

Of course, Officer Billie didn't have any idea what he was talking about. "Don't worry about your probation," she said, patting his shoulder again. "We can decide all of that later. I'll be back in touch in a week or so. Call me if you need anything." And then she was gone.

Arthur waited until the next day at lunch to tell Squeak what had happened.

"I'm awfully sorry," Squeak kept repeating about every five minutes as his glasses steamed up with tears. "I liked Mr. Hampton a lot too."

"I know. Thanks," Arthur would answer each time, and then try to change the subject to a homework question or something stupid like that.

Arthur's family wouldn't leave him alone after they heard the news. Officer Billie had called Arthur's mom at work on Tuesday to tell her. She came home early—a rare occurrence.

"I can't believe all of this happened so suddenly. You just saw Mr. Hampton on Saturday, didn't you?" Arthur's mom said, giving him a hug when she got home.

Which didn't help much.

On Friday, Roger invited him to a Washington Senators baseball game to take his mind off things. When Arthur turned him down, he suggested bowling, then a movie.

"I really don't want to do anything, no matter what it is," Arthur finally told Roger. "Thanks."

Barbara left a bunch of rainbow drawings on his bed and insisted on giving him the silver bead from Mr. Hampton to keep. "So you can remember your friend," she said.

Which was really sweet of her, Arthur thought, even if seeing the silver temperature knob from the toaster almost made him bust up and start crying.

FORTY-TWO

On Saturday, Arthur went to see Groovy Jim. He didn't really want to go, but he wasn't sure if Groovy Jim had heard about Mr. Hampton, and he wanted to check what was happening with the garage.

So she wouldn't worry, he told his mom he was going to the library to look up something for a school project.

"What's the project?" she asked.

Arthur scrambled to come up with something. "Parts of the cell."

His mom didn't look as if she believed him, but she let him go.

"Hey, kiddo, you're here early," Groovy Jim said cheerfully when Arthur walked in. He was eating a bowl of popcorn, even though it was only ten o'clock in the morning. "What's up?"

Right then, Arthur knew the guy hadn't heard.

Arthur tugged at the front of his hair nervously. Now that he was standing there, he didn't want to be the one to tell Groovy Jim the news. He wasn't even sure how to start. He hated using words like *died* or *passed away*.

"It's about Mr. Hampton," he said slowly.

Groovy Jim looked at Arthur, his face suddenly serious. "What's wrong? Has something happened to him?" When Arthur didn't answer right away, he said, "Jeez oh pete. He's gone, isn't he?"

"Yes," Arthur mumbled.

Standing up, Groovy Jim slowly walked to the front window of his shop. He stood there for a few minutes, shaking his head and rubbing his eyes.

"When did it happen?" he asked finally.

"Tuesday morning," Arthur answered.

"Man, I can't believe it," he said, staring out the window. "I just can't believe it. I hadn't seen Hampton around this week, but I didn't think anything was wrong. That crazy old man was such a good guy. A real good guy."

Arthur had no idea why he chose this moment to admit what he'd done to Mr. Hampton, but the confession came pouring out before he could stop it.

"You know, I was the kid who hit him last fall," he blurted out. "That's why I was working for him."

Groovy Jim's reaction took him by surprise. The guy turned around and gave a sly smile. "Don't worry, kiddo. I knew who you were the minute you walked into my shop back in December. I was in court the day you were sentenced. I drove Hampton to the courthouse. Told him I'd be there to support him."

Arthur stared at Groovy Jim in disbelief. He'd been in court the day he was sentenced? He knew the whole story?

"Why didn't you ever tell me that?"

Groovy Jim shrugged. "You didn't say anything to me, did you? So I guess we all have our secrets, don't we?"

Arthur had to admit this was true.

There was a lot he'd kept from Groovy Jim.

Groovy Jim went back to his chair behind the counter and sat down, still looking shaken up by the news. Finally, he said, "Well, thanks for coming here to tell me about Hampton, kiddo. I know it wasn't an easy thing to do."

Arthur reached into his pocket for the piece of paper he had brought along. "I have something else to ask you." He glanced in the direction of the garage. "I promised Mr. Hampton I wouldn't let anything happen to his artwork. So I was wondering if you could let me know if someone comes to move it or something?" he said, holding out the folded paper. "I wrote my number down for you here."

Groovy Jim looked surprised. "Nobody knows what's happening with his stuff?"

Arthur shook his head. "No."

He'd tried asking Officer Billie about it, he told Groovy Jim. The day before, he'd called to tell her again how Mr. Hampton had left some "very important projects" in his garage and was worried about what would happen to them. But she'd insisted there wasn't much she could do. "Unless Mr.

Hampton wrote his wishes down, these things are complicated," she'd said.

"So are there any plans for a funeral or memorial for him?" Groovy Jim asked.

Arthur said he'd heard that there were some relatives in South Carolina, where Mr. Hampton was from, and he might be buried there—but that was all he knew.

Groovy Jim sighed. "Too bad he didn't have family here."

"Yeah," Arthur agreed.

There was another long silence.

"So you'll let me know if anything happens, right?" he repeated.

Groovy Jim nodded. "Don't worry. I'll keep an eye on things. The project meant a lot to Hampton. I know you worked hard on it too."

But Arthur watched nervously as Groovy Jim shoved the folded piece of paper under his cash register drawer. Would he remember where he'd put the number? Would he watch the garage like he said? Would he call?

Arthur knew he couldn't be there twenty-four hours a day. He couldn't stand guard over the artwork. Trust didn't come easily to him, but he had to trust Groovy Jim would do what he said.

A few days later, Groovy Jim kept his promise.

"Someone called for you," Arthur's sister announced when he came in from shooting baskets outside. She was mixing a pitcher of Tang in the kitchen. Although he'd only been outside for a short time, she'd already managed to spill powder and ice cubes everywhere.

"Who was it?" Arthur asked, getting annoyed by the mess.

His sister looked upward. "I think he said his name was Gloomy Jim."

It took a minute for Arthur to register what his sister was saying. "You mean *Groovy* Jim?"

She shrugged. "I guess."

Arthur's heart began to pound. "What did he say?"

"He said you need to come to the garage right away because something is happening." Barbara put her hands on her hips, squinting suspiciously at Arthur. "Who's Gloomy Jim and what garage is he talking about?"

"I'll tell you later," he said.

After making his sister promise she'd stay inside while he was gone, he took off running, desperately hoping he wasn't too late.

FORTY-THREE

Everything had been moved.

Arthur's heart nearly stopped when he reached the gravel alley and saw what was happening.

Mr. Hampton had always said, *Don't. Move. Anything.* Everything in his creation had its place. Everything had been perfectly balanced.

But Arthur could see that the big corrugated metal door at the front of the garage—the door that had never been open—was pushed up. Cardboard boxes of unused foil and glass bottles and mirrors sat on the gravel outside, waiting to be hauled away. The fragile pieces of Mr. Hampton's masterpiece had been moved to the sides of the garage.

"STOP!" Arthur tore down the alleyway, his arms flailing wildly in the air, as Groovy Jim and another man stepped outside.

"What are you doing?" Arthur's voice was a shriek. He

could feel the veins pounding in his forehead. His face felt like it was on fire. *"Can't you see that is someone's work of art?"* he shouted, pointing at the masterpiece. *"That's heaven! Everything in there is supposed to be heaven!"*

Groovy Jim stepped closer to Arthur. "Okay, kiddo, you've got to calm down," he said as he squeezed Arthur's shoulder. "I know you're upset about the stuff being moved. It wasn't anybody's fault. I only got here a few minutes ago myself. Just calm down a little and I know we can work this out."

"I don't want to calm down." Arthur yanked his shoulder out of Groovy Jim's grip. "You were supposed to watch the garage!" he shouted.

"All right, well, let's just talk things over with this guy. I'm sure we can figure something out." Groovy Jim turned toward the other man and introduced Arthur to him. "Arthur, this is Tony. He's the landlord who owns the garage."

It took a minute for those words to sink in. The guy in front of him *owned* the garage.

"Hey, kid." The landlord looked at Arthur uneasily—as if he was afraid he might completely flip out. "I didn't mean to upset you. I had no clue what the things in the garage were. I just came here to clean up the place and get it ready for renting out. I didn't know it was some guy's stuff."

"It's the Throne of the Third Heaven," Arthur shot back. "Not 'some guy's stuff.' "

The landlord looked like a gangster. Greased-back dark hair. A thick gold chain around his neck. Fake smile. Arthur didn't believe a word he was saying.

"Arthur worked on the project with the man who died," Groovy Jim explained. "He was kind of second in charge of creating the masterpiece with him."

The landlord looked at the two of them like they were lunatics. "The thing is made out of junk, right?" he said, glancing back at the pieces in the garage as if he wasn't quite sure they were talking about the same thing.

"First off, it's not junk," Arthur said, his voice rising. "It started on an island in World War II. With things from an island. It started with Death and War." His voice grew louder and shakier, and he could tell he was on the verge of losing it.

Jamming his hands in his pockets, he stared at the gravel under his feet. He had to get a grip. He was the Director of Special Projects for the State of Eternity. Mr. Hampton was counting on him. He couldn't fall apart.

"Look," the landlord said impatiently. "I don't know what the hell the old guy was building here. You say it's supposed to be some masterpiece. I have no idea what's art and what's not. It looks like junk to me, but I'm no judge. You pay the rent and I don't care what you do. You can build whatever crazy stuff you want."

"The Throne of the Third Heaven," Arthur said again. "Not stuff."

"How much?" Groovy Jim asked.

The landlord crossed his thick arms. "Hampton paid fifty a month. But April and May weren't paid up, so I'll need a hundred for back rent. After that, it's fifty a month."

Arthur's heart sank. One hundred dollars. And then fifty a month after that? Where would he get that kind of cash?

Groovy Jim asked, "If I give you fifty right now, could you give us a week or two to figure out what we want to do next? Given the circumstances and all."

Arthur's eyes darted toward Groovy Jim. He didn't think he had that kind of money.

"Sure, I'm a reasonable guy." The landlord nodded.

For a gangster, Arthur thought.

Feeling guilty that he didn't even have a dollar to contribute, Arthur watched as Groovy Jim emptied all the cash from his wallet and gave it to the guy. Then he had to go and clean out the cash register in his shop and the spare change jar on the counter to finally make it to fifty bucks.

"Take until the end of May to make up your minds," the man said, shoving the handful of bills and coins into his pants pocket.

The end of May was less than three weeks away.

"And I'm sorry again for messing up the guy's work," he added. "I'm just a regular guy who rents out buildings. I don't know much about art and culture and stuff like that, okay?"

Arthur almost believed the guy was sorry. He would have believed it for sure if the guy hadn't taken all of Groovy Jim's money.

"You'll leave everything alone until the end of May?" he asked the landlord, just to be sure. "You won't come back?"

"Not unless you burn the place down, kid," the guy joked.

Arthur didn't even crack a smile.

After the landlord finally left in his rattling truck, Arthur turned to Groovy Jim. "He took all your money," he said, feeling sick.

Groovy Jim shook his head and laughed. "No big deal. It's not the first time somebody's taken all my money. Probably won't be the last time either. Now, let's get heaven put back together."

They started rebuilding Mr. Hampton's creation as carefully as they could. The gold throne chair with its big set of shimmering wings was first. Around it, they arranged the dozens of intricate tables and pedestals and pillars. Arthur remembered where a lot of the pieces went, and he thought Squeak, being Squeak, would probably remember even more.

Luckily, a lot of the bigger pieces had wheels on them, which was something he had never noticed before.

Heaven on wheels, Arthur thought. His dad would have loved the idea.

FORTY-FOUR

Unfortunately, Arthur had no luck asking Officer Billie for help with the landlord. He wasn't sure why he'd bothered. He should have known better.

He called the officer when he got home—after paying off his sister to keep quiet with a box of Good & Plenty candy he'd been saving. He hoped Officer Billie would still be at work, even though it was just after five.

As usual, she answered on the first ring. But she sounded annoyed by his phone call, especially when he told her how he'd run into the landlord at Mr. Hampton's old garage.

"And why were you at the garage in the first place?" she interrupted. "Mr. Hampton's possessions aren't your concern. We've discussed this already."

"Well, then whose concern are they?" Arthur was surprised by his boldness.

Officer Billie sighed loudly. "I don't know. I told you these situations take a long time. Family members have to be located. The court might need to get involved."

"But what if the landlord sells what's in the garage? Or throws it out?" Arthur knew he sounded kind of crazed and desperate. "I don't think he cares about Mr. Hampton's things at all."

"I'm surprised you do," Officer Billie replied.

Arthur ignored her and kept going. "Could you at least talk to Judge Warner? Maybe there's something he can do to stop the landlord."

Even as the words left his mouth, he couldn't believe he was asking for Judge Warner's help—the same judge who would have put him in juvie for months, maybe years, if it had been up to him. But judges could make rulings about things, couldn't they? That's what they did in the movies. Arthur knew he was grasping at straws, but he was out of ideas.

"I'll look into it. That's all I'm promising," Officer Billie said firmly. "I'll be speaking to the judge soon about your probation hours and what we're going to do about them. I'll see what he says. In the meantime, stay out of trouble. Don't take anything that doesn't belong to you, is that clear?"

No. Nothing was clear to Arthur anymore.

FORTY-FIVE

"You're trying to save what?" Arthur's mom asked, looking confused.

Since Officer Billie hadn't been of much use, Arthur had decided to ask his mom and Roger for help. He was running out of time to pay the last fifty dollars of the back rent. The end of May was approaching fast. Squeak had offered the thirty dollars he was saving for college, but they would still be short, especially since they needed to come up with the rent for June now too.

So he'd waited until they were all sitting around the kitchen table for their usual Friday-night dinner. Arthur's mom was in the middle of serving a peach cobbler for dessert. It was a little burned on the bottom, so she was preoccupied with that, but Arthur decided he'd bring up Mr. Hampton's project anyhow.

"I'm trying to save something Mr. Hampton was working on before he died," Arthur said, just to get things started. He didn't say it was supposed to represent heaven. Or that it was made of junk. He described it as a gold-and-silver sculpture built with a lot of different objects.

"It fills half of a garage. It's really spectacular," he added, trying to make the work of art sound great.

Arthur's mom looked up from cutting the peach cobbler. "I didn't know Mr. Hampton was an artist. I thought he was more of a junk collector."

Arthur nodded. "Well, yeah, some of the junk was for his sculptures."

"Why would he make sculptures out of junk?" Barbara asked.

Arthur could tell the conversation was already getting off track. "Anyway, I'm trying to save his artwork," he pushed on. "But the garage where he stored everything costs fifty dollars a month to rent."

"Fifty dollars a month? For a *garage*?" Arthur's mom looked shocked.

"Oh, so that's why you went to the garage!" Barbara blurted out.

"Why is it in a garage?" Roger asked. "Couldn't it be moved somewhere else?"

"Somewhere that doesn't cost so much," Arthur's mom added.

Arthur thought about all the delicate pieces—the hundreds of fragile lightbulbs wrapped in foil, the wings attached with pieces of coffee cans and nails and pins. He shook his head. "I don't think it would work—"

"Well, people can't expect you to pay for a garage by

yourself," his mom interrupted. "That wasn't part of your probation sentence. You're thirteen years old. We don't have that kind of money. Isn't there someone else who could take over instead? Officer Billie said Mr. Hampton had some family in South Carolina. . . ."

"Nobody else is going to understand what he did. That's what I'm trying to tell you."

Arthur could feel his frustration growing. Why didn't *anybody* get what he was saying?

"I'm the one he put in charge of everything. I'm the only one who really knows what it is." His voice rose and he could see his mom giving one of her warning looks, but he couldn't stop.

"I worked on it for months," he continued, even louder. "Every Saturday, that's what I did—I worked on collecting things and making things for it. In the snow and rain and everything." Arthur's voice shook. "And if people don't get what it's supposed to be—and how important it is—they'll probably go and throw it out before anybody can say anything—"

Instantly, Arthur regretted those words.

A hurt look passed across his mom's face, and she stood up from the table and walked straight out of the kitchen.

Barbara's mouth was a little O.

Roger looked confused by the whole scene. Arthur wasn't sure how much of the story of his dad's hat and the brick he knew.

And honestly, the connection hadn't crossed Arthur's

mind until it was too late. He'd just said the first thing that came into his head. Which was always a mistake.

"I better go see where Mom went," he mumbled, feeling his face get warm as he slowly got up from the table.

"You're in big trouble," Barbara said.

"Just shut up." He glared at his sister as he walked out.

Arthur found his mom upstairs, sitting on her bed, holding a box of tissues in her lap. Her neck and cheeks had bright red blotches on them. She always broke out in blotches when she was upset. He felt like a total jerk.

"I'm sorry, Mom," he said, standing awkwardly in the doorway, as if there were an invisible DO NOT CROSS line there. "I didn't mean what I said. I wasn't talking about you throwing out Dad's things. That's not what I meant."

"It sounded like what you meant."

Arthur sighed loudly. "It wasn't. I was just trying to talk about Mr. Hampton's work, and nobody was listening."

"I was listening. I heard everything you said," his mom insisted. "But you can't save everything, Artie. Sometimes in life you have to let things go." She fidgeted with the tissue in her hands. "That's all I was doing with your dad's things. I was trying to let go of some things and start over. Maybe I didn't do it the right way, but I wasn't trying to hurt you or your dad. I loved him just as much as you did, you know?" She looked up at him, her eyes welling with tears, and Arthur wished he could disappear. He couldn't stand seeing his mom cry.

"Okay." He tugged at his hair. "I get what you mean." Then he added, "But I can't really let go of the stuff with Mr. Hampton. I kind of promised him I wouldn't."

"And people expect you to save his artwork all by yourself?" His mom looked doubtful.

Arthur shrugged.

"I just can't believe that would be true."

"Well, it is."

"All right. Then here," his mom said with an impatient sigh. Reaching into the tissue box in her lap, she pulled out two wrinkled ten-dollar bills. "You can have your birthday money early." Arthur's birthday was in June. "It's up to you if you want to use it for the garage."

"You keep my birthday money in a *Kleenex* box?" Arthur said as he took the bills from his mom. "Why?"

"Because you make me cry a lot, why else?" his mom retorted. Then a small smile crept across her blotchy face. "And that way I never forget where it is."

For some reason, this made both of them crack up.

THE SIXTH IMPORTANT THING

Even though they now had enough cash to cover the back rent with Arthur's birthday money, Squeak's college money, and Groovy Jim's fifty bucks, they still needed to pay for June. And what would happen after that? Arthur knew they couldn't keep renting the garage forever. So where would Mr. Hampton's work go?

School was impossible. In his notebooks, Arthur made lists of questions he wished he'd asked Mr. Hampton. He tried to come up with ways he could earn money to pay the rent. He sketched wings and stars all over his book covers. It was a good thing there were only a couple more weeks of school left and the teachers weren't giving out much work, because he probably would have failed everything.

In the middle of earth science one afternoon, Mr. C asked him a question about metamorphic rocks from a chapter they were reading in class, and Arthur looked up from one of his wing drawings and said, "I don't know and I don't care."

This was the truth. He didn't give a crap about metamorphic rocks. All he cared about was Hampton's Throne, which was sitting in a crummy garage and could be destroyed in days—or weeks—if he couldn't find a way to save it.

Of course, his comment got him sent straight to the vice principal's office, without passing Go.

It was while he was slouching in one of the office chairs waiting on Vice that Mr. Hampton sent a message to him.

Well, not a real message—a subliminal kind of message.

Arthur was trying not to make eye contact with the secretaries, who were giving him random disapproving glares from their desks, when he noticed something familiar sitting on the counter nearby.

Most Important Thing #6: Coffee cans.

He'd collected dozens of them during the months that he'd worked for Mr. Hampton. The sides were cut into strips. Then the curved metal pieces were used like hinges to attach the cardboard angel wings to everything.

Arthur could see Mr. Hampton's idea for him almost immediately.

The coffee can in the office was decorated with red construction paper. On the front, in not very neat printing, it said: Donate to the Band Uniform Fund—with a bunch of musical notes drawn all over the rest of the paper. In the top was a slot where you could put your money.

One of the secretaries noticed Arthur staring at the coffee can. She stood up and moved it off the counter, out of reach.

"Don't get any ideas," she said in a snippy voice.

"Sure," Arthur replied, hardly able to hold back the big fat smile that was trying to slide across his face.

It was too late, he wanted to tell the secretary. He already had the idea he needed.

FORTY-SIX

After school the next day, Squeak and Arthur gathered all of the unused coffee cans Hampton had left in his garage, lined them up in the middle of the floor, and counted them. There were thirty-two.

If they only collected four or five bucks in each one, they'd have enough money to pay for June and July. And if they were lucky, maybe even August.

"That's nothing," Squeak said. "We can do it."

The hard part was deciding what message to put on them. Words were not Arthur's strength. He suggested "Help Us Save Heaven" to get everybody's attention. "Who could ignore that?"

Squeak tried to be diplomatic. "People might not understand what 'saving heaven' means. They might think you're talking about some kind of religious experience."

"Well, how would you describe it, then?" Arthur waved

his arm impatiently toward Hampton's creation, glimmering gently in the light and shadows of the room. He felt like they were wasting precious time. They only had until supper to work on the cans.

Squeak was quiet for a moment, studying the captivating scene again. It had a power that was hard to describe, no matter how many times you saw it. "How about 'Help Save a Unique Artistic Masterpiece from Destruction'?" he finally said.

"Get real." Arthur rolled his eyes. "Nobody is going to read all that junk on a coffee can."

Looking hurt, Squeak blinked fast behind his glasses.

"How about just 'Help Save a Work of Art'?" Arthur suggested more gently. He knew Squeak was only trying to help—unlike Arthur, he had a big chemistry test to cram for that night.

"People probably aren't going to care enough about saving a work of art," Squeak insisted. "It sounds . . ." He paused. "Ordinary."

Arthur let out a frustrated sigh. "Well, then give me something better. You're the word person."

"Unique. How about 'Save a Unique Work of Art'?" Squeak suggested.

And then he continued tossing out words like a crazed word machine as he walked back and forth past the Throne of the Third Heaven. "Cool. Magical. Spectacular. One of a kind. Brilliant. Original. Priceless. Breathtaking. Intense. Sparkling. Awesome. Surreal—"

"Nobody is going to know what the heck *surreal* means," Arthur interrupted.

"I do," Squeak insisted stubbornly.

"Well, I don't."

They ended up making each coffee can different.

Squeak wrote the words in marker on construction paper—borrowed from Arthur's sister—because he had neater printing and way better spelling than Arthur. Then Arthur glued the paper onto each can. It was hard not to think about Mr. Hampton while they were gluing and decorating. Arthur knew he would have liked the fact that they added bits of foil to the labels for some sparkle.

Each coffee can had a different message. *Save a Brilliant Work of Art. Save a Far-Out Work of Art. Save a Spectacular Work of Art.*

You couldn't tell what would appeal to people, Squeak said. They even used *heavenly* on one coffee can.

Save a Heavenly Work of Art.

Surprisingly—or maybe not surprisingly—that was the coffee can that finally paid off.

FORTY-SEVEN

They scattered the coffee cans around Washington, D.C.

Every shop in Mr. Hampton's old neighborhood got one. Groovy Jim took two. The guy who ran the grocery store across the street agreed to put one on his counter next to the Bazooka gum.

"What is this work of art about?" he asked curiously. A small, dark-skinned Indian man with a British accent, he reminded Arthur of Mr. C. "Have I seen it before?"

Arthur told the shop owner how Mr. Hampton—the old man who had pushed a grocery cart around the neighborhood for years—had been building a masterpiece in the garage across the street. And how they were trying to save it.

"Ah yes." The man nodded vigorously. "I remember him. He was an artist?"

"Yeah. A pretty good artist," Arthur said.

"Well, I will try to help." The man smiled and shrugged. "No promises, right? I will do my best. Good luck."

Squeak took some coffee cans to drop off at his dad's work and a bunch of other places. He wouldn't say where his dad worked, which Arthur thought was kind of odd, but he didn't push it. Squeak's violin teacher put one in his music store. And Squeak also managed to sweet-talk the school office ladies into setting one on the counter next to the Band Uniform Fund.

They liked Squeak a lot more than they liked Arthur.

Arthur was surprised when his mom said she'd put one in the dentist's office. His dad had never agreed with fundraising. Not even car washes. "Our family doesn't beg for money," he always said.

Of course, then Roger the Carpenter insisted on putting a couple of bucks in the *Save a Spectacular Work of Art* coffee can his mom took—just to get things started, he said.

It bugged Arthur that the guy always had to be so nice.

A week later, Squeak and Arthur met to count the money they'd collected. On Saturday, Squeak came to Arthur's house carrying a cardboard box full of jangling coffee cans.

Even before they started counting, Arthur had already figured out that the jangling noise wasn't a good sign. It meant the cans were mostly full of coins—and most of those coins were dimes, nickels, and pennies. It didn't take a math genius to figure out they'd need an awful lot of pennies and nickels to raise the money they needed.

And clearly, some people couldn't read either, because

they left crumpled gum wrappers, a cigarette butt, store receipts, and a girl's barrette in the cans.

But in the bottom of one of Squeak's coffee cans—the *Save a Heavenly Work of Art* can—they found a business card from a reporter at the city newspaper. On the other side of the card, the reporter had scrawled in pencil: *Sounds interesting, call me.*

"Where did you leave this coffee can?" Arthur asked curiously. "Do you remember?"

A strange look passed across Squeak's face. He didn't say anything. After a minute or two of weird silence, he took off his glasses and cleaned them on his shirt. Then he put them back on again, still saying nothing.

Arthur started to ask what was wrong when Squeak interrupted him and said, "All right. I have a confession to make."

"A confession?" Arthur was confused. "About the coffee can?"

Squeak sighed loudly. "I put it in the office of the newspaper where my dad works."

It took a minute for Squeak's words to sink in.

"Your dad is a reporter?" Arthur said slowly.

He hated all reporters—especially after they'd plastered his crime across every newspaper in D.C. They'd done the same thing after his dad's motorcycle accident. They'd written things about his dad's death that weren't true—or at least, things people didn't need to know about his drinking and past misdeeds.

"Why didn't you tell me your dad was a reporter?"

"No, not a reporter," Squeak jumped in quickly to explain. "A truck driver. He drives a delivery truck for the newspaper."

Arthur squinted at Squeak, trying to picture him being the son of a newspaper delivery truck driver. It wasn't what he'd imagined at all. He'd figured Squeak's parents were professors or rich people or something.

"Okay." Arthur shrugged. "So your dad drives a truck, no big deal."

"Don't you remember what happened with Mr. Hampton?" Squeak continued, looking more and more nervous. "Remember how it was a newspaper delivery truck driver who found him on the sidewalk?"

And now the truth behind Squeak's confession finally dawned on Arthur.

"That guy was your dad?"

"Yes," Squeak said, swallowing loudly. "It was."

"For real, you're not making this up?"

Squeak shook his head.

At this point, Arthur burst out laughing.

He fell back on the worn-out blue carpet of the living room, holding his stomach and laughing so hard he thought he might puke. The whole crazy train wreck of coincidences suddenly seemed ridiculously funny: Squeak's dad saves Mr. Hampton after he's been hit by Arthur. Mr. Hampton saves Arthur from juvie. Arthur saves Squeak from the trash can at school. And now here they were—trying to save Hampton's masterpiece from destruction.

"What's so funny?" Squeak's face reddened.

"Do your parents know you're hanging out with me?" Arthur said, sitting up to take a breath. He couldn't believe any parent would allow their kid to hang out with him—especially not the parent who had found Mr. Hampton with a busted arm on the sidewalk.

"Not—not really," Squeak stammered. "Well, they know about you being my friend, but I've kind of made up a different name and story for you. You're not who they think you are."

Arthur grinned. "I'm not who a lot of people think I am."

"I know," said Squeak.

"And I guess you're not who people think you are," he said with another loud snort of laughter.

"I know," said Squeak, finally starting to relax and smile. "I think that's why we get along."

Arthur picked up the business card from the carpet. "So what should we do about this reporter?"

"I think you should call him."

Although Arthur didn't really want to call, once he looked over the lousy collection of coins and bills and junk spread out on the living room carpet, he knew they didn't have much choice.

FORTY-EIGHT

When Arthur reached the reporter at the newspaper office, he seemed confused at first. "What's this about?" he said. "I'm not clear on what you're saying."

Taking a deep breath, Arthur repeated his story of how he'd found the reporter's business card in the coffee can he'd been using to raise money for a special work of art. "It said on the back that I was supposed to call you," he added.

"All right," the guy said, still sounding kind of lost. "Give me a few more details about what you're doing."

Stumbling over his explanation, Arthur started out by telling the reporter how he was trying to save an important piece of artwork made out of junk by a man who had just died.

Squeak glanced up from the coins he was counting. "Make it sound better than that!"

Trying to be more convincing, Arthur explained how the

idea for the work of art started with World War II and how it was supposed to represent heaven with a throne and wings and stars made of shiny things like old foil and mirrors. "It's in a garage here in D.C., on Seventh Street Northwest, if you know where that is," he said. "I think there are more than a hundred and fifty pieces inside the garage. But I haven't counted them all yet."

"Let me get this straight. The guy you're talking about made heaven out of shiny stuff he got from the trash?" the reporter asked, sounding dubious.

"And other things," Arthur tried to say. "Like cardboard and glass."

"And everything the guy built is inside a garage that nobody else knows about?" Arthur thought he could hear the reporter writing something down.

"No, I don't think anybody really knows about it," he answered.

"When can I see it?"

"Uh, right now, if you want to, I guess," Arthur stammered.

Despite not sounding very sure about anything, he must have been convincing enough, because the reporter said he'd be there. "I'll bring along a photographer to shoot some pictures too," he told him.

"Okay."

"I'll need an address."

"Oh yeah," Arthur said, feeling stupid. He told him, then remembered all the trouble he'd had when he first looked for the garage. "But it's kind of hard to find by the address," he added. "You can't see it from the street. It's easier to watch for a tattoo shop called Groovy Jim's and then drive down the gravel alley next to it. The garage is in the back."

"A garage behind a tattoo shop . . ."

"I'll meet you there," Arthur said. "I promise."

An hour later, Arthur and Squeak met the reporter and his photographer at the garage. The reporter was about sixty, while the photographer looked like a younger version of Groovy Jim—tall and skinny, with a rumpled shirt and slacks. He carried the biggest camera and flashbulb Arthur had ever seen, slung casually over one shoulder. He also seemed to be really fond of the words *wow* and *impressive*.

When the four of them stepped into the garage, the photographer walked straight over to Hampton's creation. "Wow. Impressive," he said. Still staring at the scene, he pulled the camera off his shoulder and started to shoot some pictures.

But the reporter's eyes swept quickly over the work of art, as if it was just another job he had to do. He snapped open his notebook and rattled off his questions like a cop.

What was the work of art made of? Who had made it? How long had it taken? What was the purpose of it? What had the artist been hoping to do with it?

Arthur couldn't answer some of the questions. He didn't know how long Mr. Hampton had worked on his creation— only that one piece had been made during World War II.

He didn't really know Hampton's purpose for the Throne either—except for being one of the few works of art to show what heaven might look like.

"It's a lot easier to show hell. Everybody has done that," he added, which made the reporter look up from his notes and give a coughing sort of laugh.

At the end of the interview, the reporter asked for Arthur's and Squeak's names.

"Spell your names for me," he said as he was wrapping up his notes for the article. "I want to mention what you two young fellows are trying to do."

So far, Arthur had been able to avoid telling the reporter who he was—about his crime and probation sentence. He hoped to keep it that way.

"Uh, I'd rather not have my name in the article, if that's okay," he mumbled. Then Squeak jumped in to add in a pseudo-innocent voice: "Actually, both of us would like our volunteer work on this project to remain anonymous."

We'd like our work to remain anonymous. Perfect, Arthur thought. Sometimes it helped to have a smart kid on your side.

"Sure, I understand." The reporter flipped his notebook closed with a loud snap. "Thanks, fellows. I'll try to get my editors to run the piece on Monday. Slow news day, usually," he said. "Good luck. Hope you find a home for the guy's work."

Next to him, the photographer looked back at the

shimmering creation again. Some of the foil-covered wings seemed to be moving a little in the warm breeze that was sweeping through the garage. There was a soft metallic-paper sound.

"Wow, I gotta say, it is a pretty impressive piece, with all those wings and everything," the photographer remarked again as he pulled his camera strap over his shoulder. "But it's kind of sad too, if you think about it . . . old guy, working on this project all those years alone. Sad."

Arthur didn't really see the sadness of the Throne of the Third Heaven, but he didn't say anything. It was what Hampton had wanted to do. A lot of people had done worse things with their lives than taking ugliness and turning it into something beautiful.

FORTY-NINE

The article came out in the newspaper on Monday. Despite its being on a back page below a column about the best ways to trim rosebushes, everybody saw it.

ECCENTRIC ARTIST BUILDS
MASTERPIECE IN GARAGE

It didn't take much for Officer Billie to guess that the "anonymous individuals collecting money to save the masterpiece" mentioned in the article probably included Arthur Owens.

She called on Monday afternoon, right after Arthur got home from school, and demanded that he give her all of the details. "I want to know exactly what you are doing and how involved you are in this project," she said. "The buck stops with me, remember?"

Arthur couldn't tell if she was mad or pleased. He had the feeling she knew more than she was letting on.

"I told you the landlord needed money," he cautiously explained. "So that's what we were trying to collect."

"And how did you do?"

"Not great," Arthur admitted. "But maybe the article will help." He and Squeak had distributed all the coffee cans around town again.

Officer Billie told him she would keep looking into things.

Arthur's mom acted as though he had saved somebody's life. "I'm so proud of you," she kept saying after she saw the article. "I had no idea what you were really talking about when you were describing that project in the garage," she said, squinting at the small photograph in the paper. "I can't believe this is what you were working on for your probation."

Arthur tried not to make a big deal of the newspaper article, but he was glad the secret was finally out. He felt as if a heavy weight had been lifted off his shoulders. People knew about Mr. Hampton's work now. As the Director of Special Projects for the State of Eternity, he'd done his job. He'd gotten the word out. Maybe other people would step in and help now.

Only that didn't happen.

It turned out just a handful of generous people dropped by the newspaper office to make small donations to the project after reading the article. Their donations amounted to less than thirty dollars.

A few visitors found the garage and stopped at Groovy Jim's shop to ask for a tour. Most of them didn't offer to leave any money for the cause.

One of the most promising visitors was a minister who was interested in Hampton's Throne for his church. But after he saw how the work of art was made of foil-covered cardboard and lightbulbs and old furniture, he didn't want it. "I don't see what you're going to do with it," he told Groovy Jim. "No church is going to want a sculpture of heaven made of trash."

Arthur was glad he hadn't been there to hear the minister's comments. He already knew time was running out. They'd scraped up enough money from the coffee cans and the other donations to pay for June and part of July, but that was all.

He kept hoping Mr. Hampton would somehow show him what to do next. He searched through every spare box of paper and tinfoil and cardboard in the garage, looking for clues from him. One Saturday, he went through the drawers in Mr. Hampton's messy workbench, thinking maybe he'd left some plans about where the Throne was supposed to go. Nothing.

He worried that he wasn't looking deep enough. *Where there is no vision, the people perish.* That had been one of Mr. Hampton's favorite sayings. So Arthur spent a lot of time sitting in front of the creation, trying to picture what he might have wanted for his work. But no matter how long Arthur stared at the masterpiece, he still couldn't see what to do with it.

Finally, Officer Billie called with some good news. A few people from an art museum were interested in seeing Hampton's work. Would Arthur be willing to give them a tour? she asked.

Not feeling very hopeful, Arthur said yes.

FIFTY

There were five people in the group—two women and three men. They came on a Saturday in two taxis. Arthur wished Squeak could have been there, but one of his cousins was getting married, so Arthur was on his own.

He didn't like being on his own. He liked it even less when he saw the group. They looked as if they had come straight from a country club. Even though it was a warm June day, the men were wearing suit coats and bow ties. The two women had on stylish dresses and high heels. They didn't seem very happy about having to walk through the trash-strewn gravel to the garage in their good shoes either.

Arthur tried to be polite—holding the door open and saying hello to everyone. But it didn't seem to matter much. Once the five people got through the doorway, they ignored him completely and headed straight for Mr. Hampton's creation.

They gathered in a tight knot in front of it, talking among

themselves. Arthur couldn't tell if they liked it or not because he couldn't hear much of what was being said. But he was kind of shocked when one of the women walked up to a silver table in the display and pulled it forward without even asking for permission.

Then she started tapping a couple of the foil-covered lightbulbs with her painted fingernails and running her hands along the decorated sides. She even kneeled down to look underneath the table.

"It's a discarded bedside table from the twenties or thirties," she said to the rest of the group. "Decorated with cardboard scraps, lightbulbs, and maybe some foil-covered Ping-Pong balls here and there. Looks like everything is held together with strips of metal cans, straight pins, and glue."

Ping-Pong balls?

Arthur shook his head. None of the Seven Most Important Things were *Ping-Pong balls.* They were crumpled balls of foil. If anybody had bothered to ask him, he could have told the group exactly what they were. He'd made some of them himself.

"But is it art?" one of the men asked. He was an older guy with thick white hair who kind of looked like Albert Einstein. "I'm having a hard time seeing the artistic value in this piece—other than the fact that it is an elaborate example of how discarded odds and ends can be transformed into a religious display."

Arthur finally spoke up, because the museum people

clearly had no clue what they were looking at and he couldn't stand listening to them any longer.

"It's called the Throne of the Third Heaven," he announced from the garage doorway. "That's what it's supposed to be."

All eyes turned toward Arthur, as if noticing him for the first time.

Arthur Owens didn't really want to go on. But he decided to show off the piece Hampton had made in the war, since it was one of his favorites. He picked up the fragile box created of broken things and tried to remember all of the details about it. The island. The war. Hampton's visions. The number 3.

"Mr. Hampton said this is supposed to be Death and War turned into something beautiful," he explained.

"I like that idea," said the second woman in the group. She took off her fancy rhinestone eyeglasses and leaned closer to study the elaborate box. "Death and War turned into something beautiful."

Arthur walked around and pointed out some of the other symbols on the tables and pedestals—the angel wings, the stars, the crowns, the "lights in the darkness" lightbulbs.

The same woman who had liked the box said she thought it was interesting that Mr. Hampton covered every object in his collection with foil.

"Reflects the viewer," someone else replied.

"So what the artist could have been saying is that heaven is supposed to reflect us, the viewers," another voice added.

This bizarre idea had never occurred to Arthur. Had Mr. Hampton really wanted his masterpiece to reflect the people looking at it? Was that why everything had to shine? He glanced at the group behind him with more interest. Maybe they did know something after all.

"Mr. Hampton called the foil and some of the other things he used the Seven Most Important Things," he added, in case that might help to explain more.

For some reason, the group found this funny.

"I have no clue why he used seven for everything, but that's what he did," Arthur finished quickly, embarrassed by the laughter.

"I can tell you why," the man with the Einstein hair said. The rest of the group nodded as if they knew the reason too. "Traditionally, seven is the number of completeness and perfection—seven days of the week, seven days of creation in the Bible, and so on."

Seven—the number of completeness and perfection.

That was when the puzzle pieces finally started to fall into place for Arthur. Mr. Hampton had wanted him to find seven things to complete the project. The building blocks, he'd called them. But Arthur had also suspected they were the building blocks of his redemption too. The seven things he needed to find for himself, for his life . . .

"Is that all?" the woman with the rhinestone glasses asked Arthur.

Looking up, Arthur realized he'd completely lost track of what he'd been saying. The whole group was staring at him, wondering what the heck was going on. Wondering why the kid had suddenly lost it and stopped talking.

"Yeah," he mumbled, still feeling kind of dazed, still thinking of the seven things. "I think that's all I know."

"So, have we seen enough?" the white-haired guy asked the other four people, who nodded.

"We'll let you know what we've decided once we've had time to talk it over with the board," the man continued.

Arthur had no idea what board the museum guy meant, but he nodded anyhow, as if the plan was fine with him. He wasn't really sure if he was allowed to agree with anything. Hampton's Throne didn't even belong to him.

The entire visit only lasted about thirty minutes. Then everybody made their way across the uneven gravel again. As Arthur watched the taxis back up and leave, he hoped he'd said the right things. He hoped Mr. Hampton would have approved.

FIFTY-ONE

Arthur's fourteenth birthday was June 26. A Friday. He told his mom all he wanted was a chocolate cake and a couple of *Mad* magazines. Nothing special.

He thought about adding that he wanted just his mom and Barbara to be there—the three of them for dinner without Roger—but he knew his mom would probably take it the wrong way. She wouldn't understand that it wasn't really about Roger being there; it was about Arthur's dad *not* being there.

So he decided to keep his mouth shut.

On Friday, Barbara woke him up. "Happy birthday! I made a birthday picture for you, wanna see?" she said, hiding the picture behind her back.

"No," Arthur said. "Go away. I want to sleep."

"Look!" She waved it in front of his face. "There's you."

She pointed at a stick figure holding a baseball bat and glove with a big *14* in purple clouds over his head.

"That's nice." Arthur tried to be patient. "Thanks. Now go away, okay? It's my birthday. I want to sleep in." He turned to face the wall.

"Do you know why you have a baseball hat and glove?"

Arthur shoved his face into the pillow. "No," he said into it. "I don't."

"Well, it's a surprise. Mom and Roger said I can't tell you," his sister replied in a loud whisper. "You'll find out soon. You can go back to sleep now. Bye."

She left the picture lying on his pillow and shuffled out of the room in her slippers.

Arthur wasn't sure how chocolate cake and *Mad* magazines got turned into a Washington Senators baseball game, but they did.

Roger took all of them to a game at D.C. Stadium that night.

Actually, it was a lot more fun than Arthur thought it would be. At first he kept thinking about his dad listening to games on the radio and felt guilty his dad wasn't there and he was. But then the Senators got a couple of hits—and they were one of the worst teams in baseball, so that was a big deal, even if they ended up losing to the Orioles.

Barbara was so excited about everything, she stood up to catch foul balls that weren't anywhere close to their seats. Whenever a ball was hit, she'd leap up and put out her hands, as if the ball would somehow drop out of the sky and land in them.

Roger finally ended up buying her a souvenir baseball. "Even though it's not your birthday," he said. "I know Arthur won't mind."

They ate hot dogs and popcorn and drank Cokes. Arthur's mom laughed a lot. Probably too much, he thought. It was kind of embarrassing. Roger wasn't *that* funny, he wanted to point out.

Then they came back and had his birthday cake around midnight. Which was cool, until Barbara stayed up and chattered for half the night because she couldn't sleep. And then had to pee the rest of the night.

Arthur saved his ticket from the game. It had been a good birthday, and he wanted to remember it.

FIFTY-TWO

Officer Billie was the one who called Arthur to tell him the news about Hampton's masterpiece. It was right before the Fourth of July holiday weekend. Roger was over for dinner, as usual. Arthur had been cutting lawns all day to earn money for the August garage rent, so he was wiped out. He didn't even move to answer the phone when it rang. His mom jumped up to get it.

Holding her hand over the receiver, she told Arthur the call was for him. "It's Officer Billie," she whispered loudly. "Tell her you'll call her back later because we're eating supper now. The casserole will get cold."

Arthur ignored his mom and the casserole. He hadn't heard from Officer Billie in weeks. And she was calling before a holiday weekend. He knew it had to be something important.

He took the phone. "It's Arthur Owens," he said, trying not to sound nervous.

"Mr. Owens, I have some news I think you will be pleased to hear."

Right then, all Arthur could hear was his heart—which sounded like it was about to fly out of his chest.

"The National Collection of Fine Arts here in Washington has decided they would like to acquire Mr. Hampton's work."

"What?" Arthur asked, not quite sure what she meant. "Acquire?"

"The museum would like to have . . . to keep the work of art."

"What?" Arthur said again, feeling dizzy.

He'd been to the national art museum only once, on a school field trip in elementary school. All he could remember was the huge gold picture frames and the marble steps. It had been like a palace. He couldn't believe Hampton's collection of foil-covered art would be in a place like that.

"They're going to put Mr. Hampton's work in the museum downtown? For everybody to see?" Arthur repeated slowly.

There was a long pause before Officer Billie said, "Well, no. Not right now."

Arthur was confused. "What do you mean, not right now?"

"For the moment, the museum is acquiring it for their storage collection."

"Storage?"

"They'll put it away until they have a place for it someday."

"Oh." Arthur pictured all of the beautiful pieces being packed away in cardboard boxes in a musty attic somewhere. Like their Christmas tree.

"How long will it be there? In storage?" he managed to ask, trying not to sound as disappointed as he was.

There was a loud, exasperated sigh from Officer Billie. "I don't know. But I thought you would be happy to hear that Mr. Hampton's work is going to one of the top museums in the country."

"But—"

"*Stop!* Are you happy the project was saved or not, Mr. Owens?"

Arthur could tell Officer Billie probably had her traffic-cop hand up.

"I guess I'm happy," he mumbled.

And actually, he was glad Mr. Hampton's work was going somewhere, so he wouldn't have to lie awake nights worrying about it any longer—and mowing lawns to pay the rent. He only wished it was going to a place where people could see it. He didn't think Mr. Hampton would want heaven packed up and left in storage. He hoped he hadn't let him down.

"Nothing in this world is perfect, right?" Officer Billie said more patiently.

"Right," Arthur agreed. He managed to resist adding—except the number seven.

"Well, that's all the information I have right now. When I hear more, I'll let you know."

"Thanks." Arthur did his best to sound grateful. He didn't want another lecture.

"You're welcome," she said. "Have a good evening."

Arthur turned back to the table to see everyone staring at him. The casserole was untouched. Nobody had moved.

"What was that all about?" Arthur's mom asked.

Arthur took a deep breath and forced himself to smile. "It was Officer Billie calling to tell me that Mr. Hampton's masterpiece is going to a museum."

FIFTY-THREE

"*Mr. Hampton's art is going to a museum?*" Squeak practically launched out of his chair in Arthur's kitchen when he told him. He'd come over for lunch after being away for the Fourth of July weekend. Of course, he'd brought his own foil-wrapped food with him.

"Yeah, I guess. That's what Officer Billie told me." Arthur shrugged, as if it were no big deal, and kept eating his ham sandwich.

"Which museum?" Squeak asked, still talking extra loudly.

"National Collection of Fine Arts."

"*One of the Smithsonians?*" Squeak shrieked. He was so loud Barbara came running from the living room to see what was going on.

"*Hampton's work is going to a Smithsonian?*" Squeak shrieked again.

"Seriously, Squeak, tone it down a little." Arthur waved his sister away. "They're just putting it in storage, not in the museum."

"Well, it's better than sitting in an old garage in an alley, isn't it?" Squeak still couldn't contain his excitement. He pushed his entire packet of vanilla cremes toward Arthur. "Here. You can have all of my cookies to celebrate," he said, patting him on the shoulder. "Congratulations!"

Smiling, Arthur shook his head.

Sometimes Squeak could be such a pinhead.

THE SEVENTH IMPORTANT THING

On the last Saturday in July, Arthur decided to take one more walk to Mr. Hampton's garage.

He knew he didn't have to go there at all. His probation was over. The judge had suspended the rest of his sentence for good behavior, and Officer Billie had officially released him from being one of her kids—with another tin of caramel corn as a gift. The landlord had rented the garage to a new tenant, and the museum people had already finished packing up Hampton's Throne. They'd been working in the garage all week, according to Groovy Jim.

But Arthur wanted to see the place one last time.

It was a beautiful summer morning. Arthur couldn't help thinking that it would have been a great day for collecting the Seven Most Important Things. In the brilliant sunlight, he could see the world as perfectly as if it was outlined. He kind of felt like he was outlined too. Arthur T. Owens against the bright blue sky.

The sun warmed Arthur's neck. He thought about how almost a whole year had gone by without his dad. He felt like a different person. It felt like a different life.

Would the judge call this redemption? He wasn't sure.

He was definitely taller and stronger now. Maybe that was what pushing a grocery cart through the snow and sleet for months did to a person. A lot of his clothes didn't fit anymore. He was starting to get pale wisps of hair on his upper lip, he'd noticed, and that was funny and weird at the same time.

A lot of things were funny and weird to him these days. Like being the Director of Special Projects for the State of Eternity. He'd never told anyone about the title Mr. Hampton had given him before he died—not even Squeak—but remembering it always made Arthur feel secretly proud, as if he had a superhero side nobody knew about.

Maybe because he was so lost in his own thoughts, the walk to the garage seemed a lot shorter than it usually did.

In no time at all, Arthur was standing outside the familiar corrugated door with the drippy address numbers. The morning sunlight had just reached the garage. It glinted off the three glass bottles of Nesbitt's soda still pouring out their guilt and regrets onto the ground.

Arthur was glad to see that the landlord hadn't gotten rid of them yet.

Taking a deep breath, he pulled Mr. Hampton's keys out of his pocket and opened the door. He knew the garage would be empty when he switched on the lights. He had prepared himself for the emptiness. Still, it was a shock to see almost nothing left in the space where Hampton's shimmering, heavenly creation had once been.

The first thought that whispered through Arthur's mind was that maybe it had never been there. Maybe he had imagined the whole thing.

Don't be stupid, he told himself. Of course it had been there.

He walked slowly across the cement floor, noticing how his footsteps—even his breathing—seemed to echo loudly in the emptiness.

The museum people had left a few things piled in one corner of the garage. There were some boxes of broken mirrors and bottles and lightbulbs Mr. Hampton hadn't used. And his office chair. And the familiar grocery cart.

It was the shopping cart that got to Arthur the most.

It's a chariot, Mr. Hampton had told Barbara. *You just can't see the horses.*

Arthur knew there was no way he could leave the rust-bucket cart behind. Not after he had pushed the thing around the neighborhood for months. Not when he knew exactly where to kick the right front wheel to make it turn. Not when he had finally figured out how to get the bone-rattling noise to stop by putting heavy stuff in the bottom of the cart first. (Surprisingly, a couple of bricks came in handy for this.)

Arthur tugged Hampton's chariot from behind the boxes.

He knew his mother would have a fit about keeping a rusty grocery cart in their garage. He'd have to come up with some excuse about storing his basketballs in it or something.

As Arthur pushed the cart across the cement floor, he took one last look around.

It was hard to leave the place, even if it was just a run-down garage at the end of an alley.

He wished he knew whether he'd done the right thing. He wished Mr. Hampton had given him more directions before he died, or told him what to do. Had he saved the artwork or ruined it? he wondered. Would anybody ever see Mr. Hampton's unbelievable creation again?

And that was when Arthur noticed the square piece of cardboard in the middle of the garage floor.

It looked like the torn flap of a box.

He shook his head, thinking there was no way the cardboard was a message from Mr. Hampton. It was just a scrap that had been left behind by the museum people when they were packing up. Some piece they had forgotten.

Still, he couldn't resist picking up the piece and looking at it. Just to check. Just to be sure.

On the other side, he found seven letters carefully cut out of silver metallic foil and glued on the cardboard, which had been covered with purple paper. Arthur's breath caught in his throat as he read them.

The seven letters spelled out two words:

SEVEN YEARS LATER

Arthur didn't want to wear a suit to the reception. His mom insisted.

"This is a big deal," she said. "I don't care if you are too grown-up for me to fuss over anymore. I want you looking nice. I want to be proud of you."

She tugged on the sleeves of the new dark blue suit jacket and smoothed the fabric across his broad shoulders. He was twenty-one now and as tall as his father had been, and he had his father's stubbornness about getting dressed up for anything.

"There. It fits you perfectly. Look." Arthur's mom spun him around to face the mirror in the bathroom. "You are handsome enough to make me cry." Her voice trembled a little, and Arthur rolled his eyes.

"Please, Mom."

"Roger, Barbara—come look at Arthur," his mom called before he could stop her.

Of course Roger had to stick his head in the tiny bathroom, with Barbara right behind him. They were both decked out for the occasion too. Barbara was wearing a yellow dress with a big summer hat and white gloves—which Arthur thought was a little over the top, but she was fourteen and you couldn't tell her anything these days.

"Now all you need is a nice girl to marry, Artie," she teased.

"Oh, you be quiet," his mom scolded.

Actually, Arthur did have a nice girl he was dating. Her name was Carol, and he'd met her at the city college where he was taking a couple of classes in design and architecture. But he wasn't spilling the beans about going out with her. Not yet.

Which was typical of Arthur.

"Jiminy, everybody looks awfully sharp," Roger said. Like Arthur, he was wearing a suit—the same one he'd worn when he'd married Arthur's mom at the courthouse four years before. Arthur had been his best man.

"Are you sure I look all right?" Arthur's mom peered anxiously into the bathroom mirror. She was wearing too much blue eye shadow and her hair was piled kind of high on her head, but Arthur told her she looked perfect.

The four of them got into Roger's white Cadillac to go to the reception. He'd had the whitewalls scrubbed and the leather seats cleaned. The car smelled of lemons. Arthur would have preferred to drive there himself, but his mom wanted all of them to arrive together. He suspected she was afraid he wouldn't show up on time. The reception started at six, and Arthur was always late.

The first person Arthur spotted when they pulled into the parking lot downtown was Squeak, which made him relax a little. Arthur had invited him, and he'd driven down from Boston to be there. He was heavier and rounder now, with thicker black glasses. But he was still Squeak. Once Roger had the car safely in the space, Arthur leaped out to flag him down.

"Squeak! Squeak!"

Squeak looked confused, then embarrassed.

"You made it!" Arthur said, pounding him on the back. "Good to see you, man!" They hadn't seen each other much since the end of high school. Squeak was going to Boston College, majoring in physics. Of course.

"Reginald. Not *Squeak*," Squeak said, smiling wider. "I wouldn't have recognized you. You look like a preacher or something in that fancy suit."

"I know." Arthur grinned. "I feel like an idiot in it."

"So, you excited for tonight?" Squeak pointed at the entrance of the art museum, where a crowd of well-dressed people was already lined up on the wide steps, waiting for the reception. A colorful banner saying HAMPTON'S THRONE, OPENING SOON flapped in the warm evening breeze.

"I'm not sure yet," replied Arthur. Which was the truth.

• • •

It had been seven years since he'd last seen Hampton's Throne. Seven years since he'd been a juvenile delinquent with a probation officer. Seven years since he'd gone around the neighborhood collecting the Seven Most Important Things with a grocery cart. More than seven years since his dad had died.

It was so long ago it didn't even feel like his own life when he thought about it.

But he knew there would be a few people at the reception to remind him.

Groovy Jim was there. Arthur had called the shop to let him know about the event, and he could already spot him in the crowd—a tall, hippieish guy with his mop of curly hair pulled back in a neat ponytail.

Arthur's mom had tracked down Officer Billie, who was now working as a security guard. "She did a lot to help you," Arthur's mom reminded him. "I think we should try to let her know."

Officer Billie told Arthur's mom she'd already heard about the exhibit opening.

Of course, Arthur thought. She knew *everything*.

Officer Billie said she was pretty sure Judge Warner would be there, because he was a board member of the museum. But Arthur couldn't believe the story when he heard it from his mom. A board member? Judge Warner had seemed like the last person on earth who would be interested in art.

The rest of the people in the crowd were strangers to Arthur—museum staff and patrons and guests. People who had a lot of money to spare, by the looks of their stylish clothes and jewelry.

Arthur was suddenly glad his mother had insisted on the suit.

The museum had asked Arthur to be part of the ribbon-cutting group for the opening of the exhibit. There were five people in the group. One of them turned out to be Judge Warner. He was introduced as the Honorable Philip Warner, a board member and lifelong friend of the museum. Just as Officer Billie had said.

"From brick throwing to ribbon cutting," the judge whispered to Arthur with a half smile as he handed out the scissors to everyone. "Now, that's what I call redemption."

Even seven years later, he could still make Arthur nervous.

On the count of seven—Arthur's suggestion—they cut the silver ribbon across the entrance to the exhibit. Cameras flashed as the bits of ribbon fluttered to the floor. The crowd watching in the hallway clapped.

And then it was time to walk through the wide marble doorway to see Mr. Hampton's masterpiece on display for the first time.

This was the moment Arthur had been most afraid of.

He was worried Hampton's Throne would look smaller

and less spectacular than he remembered, the way things from your past often did. Had the pieces really filled half of a garage once? Would people understand why heaven had been made out of junk? Would they see what Hampton had been trying to do?

He didn't need to worry.

As the crowd entered the room behind him, there was a soft gasp. Arthur's breath caught in his throat. Mr. Hampton's masterpiece looked far better, far more beautiful, than he remembered.

In the darkened room, the red chair Arthur had found for Mr. Hampton years before filled the center like a radiant throne. Around it, the foil-wrapped tables and chairs and pedestals and pillars sparkled in the spotlights. Metallic wings stretched outward. Stars caught the light. And at the top of it all—above the glittering thrones and tables and pillars—was the small cardboard sign Arthur wanted everyone to see: FEAR NOT.

For a long time, Arthur stood at the side of the room watching as the museum guests filed in. He noticed how they spoke in hushed whispers as they entered the darkened space, and how they stepped forward to look at the intricate pieces more closely—then back, as if trying to grasp the scene from a distance. Forward and back. Forward and back. Like a dance.

Arthur found it hard to resist pointing out to people that there was no way of seeing everything—no matter how close or far away you were from Mr. Hampton's work. Or how many hours you stared at it. Some things in this world were meant to remain a mystery.

The line to see Hampton's Throne stretched out the door and down the hallway. It moved slowly.

And just as Mr. Hampton had said, the people kept coming.

At the reception later, Officer Billie came over to give Arthur a round metal tin. "I've switched from caramel corn to cookies," she told him. "Chocolate chip. Hope you like them."

"Thank you," Arthur said, remembering to make eye contact and sound grateful. He'd learned a few things from Officer Billie seven years earlier.

Groovy Jim stopped by to tell Arthur and Squeak that they should come and get a tattoo at his shop sometime. "I can always use the business," he joked.

"Hey, I just got one," Squeak said, rolling up his sleeve to show it off. "Look."

Groovy Jim and Arthur had to squint to see what it was. It looked like a tiny smudge of letters on his biceps: $F = ma$.

"Newton's second law of motion." Squeak prodded Arthur: "Force equals mass times acceleration. Remember that from high school?"

"Oh yeah." Arthur laughed. "Man, I cannot believe you did that. I thought you were going to get something big and scary. That's what you always said."

Squeak grinned. "Trust me, getting this little thing was scary enough."

Arthur and Squeak stayed until the end of the reception. It seemed like everybody had heard how they were the ones who had saved the Throne. People kept coming over to ask them what Mr. Hampton had been like and what they'd done. Arthur figured he and Squeak must have told the story of the coffee cans ten or fifteen times.

When Arthur and his family finally left the museum that night with the last of the guests, it was dark outside. As they came out, he couldn't help noticing the big flock of city pigeons that had gathered on the museum steps for the night. There must have been fifty birds, he thought.

As the group started down the steps, the flock suddenly took off together, moving upward like one big cloud. Everyone stopped to watch them. You could hear the beat of their noisy wings lifting into the night sky—dozens upon dozens of metallic-paper wings rising over the city.

Arthur smiled as he watched the birds disappear into the darkness, remembering his dad again, remembering what Mr. Hampton had said:

Some angels are like peacocks.

Others are less flashy. Like city pigeons.

It all depends on the wings.

AUTHOR'S NOTE

This book began about twenty-five years ago when I visited a small folk art museum in Williamsburg, Virginia. I remember stepping into a darkened exhibit room, and there it was—a breathtaking world of gold-and-silver tables and thrones and pillars.

The scene was lonely, curious, and awe-inspiring, all at the same time. It wasn't until I walked closer that I realized what the art was actually made from and saw its mysterious title: *The Throne of the Third Heaven of the Nations' Millennium General Assembly.*

The artwork and its unusual story have remained in my imagination ever since.

Today, James Hampton's masterpiece, which is sometimes referred to as *The Throne of the Third Heaven* or *Hampton's Throne*, is on permanent exhibit in Washington, D.C., at the Smithsonian American Art Museum, formerly called the

National Collection of Fine Arts. It has also traveled around the country for special exhibits. You can read more about James Hampton and the little we know about his work on the Smithsonian's website: americanart.si.edu.

Like the character in the book, James Hampton was a solitary man who created his vision of heaven in an unheated garage over many years. One hundred eighty objects make up *The Throne*. They are built of various scraps he gathered from the Seventh Street neighborhood near the garage and from government buildings in Washington, D.C., where he worked as a night janitor.

Discarded furniture, foil, glass bottles, mirrors, coffee

cans, cardboard, and lightbulbs are among the materials he used most often, which inspired the idea for the Seven Most Important Things. One piece in the collection is labeled as having been made in 1945 on Guam, where James Hampton was stationed during World War II, though the story about its meaning is my own interpretation.

Interestingly, Hampton wrote down some of his ideas and

visions in elaborately coded notebooks, which have never been deciphered.

For the purpose of the story, I used a grocery cart as James Hampton's "chariot," although he was more commonly seen pulling a child's wagon or carrying a burlap sack. The characters of Arthur Owens, Groovy Jim, and Officer Billie are fictional. Unlike the landlord in the book, the real landlord played a role in helping to save the artwork after Hampton died in early November 1964 following a long battle with cancer.

While some details about James Hampton and his work were changed for the story, others are true to life. He did refer to himself in his writings as "St. James" and the "Director of Special Projects for the State of Eternity." Wings and stars were important symbols in his designs. The quote "Where there is no vision, the people perish" was found on a bulletin board in his garage. "Fear not" appears at the top of his masterpiece.

Anonymous individuals really did contribute money to save the artwork after Hampton's death. And *The Throne* was kept in storage for seven years before going on exhibit— where it continues to intrigue and inspire visitors today.

The rest is left to the imagination.

ACKNOWLEDGMENTS

Special thanks to the important people who made this book possible: my wonderful editor, Nancy Siscoe; my agent extraordinaire, Steven Malk; copy editor Colleen Fellingham; ace proofreader Amy Schroeder; designers Kate Gartner and Trish Parcell; and my husband, Mike, who always reads the first words. Thanks also to Marcy Lindberg, Bob Kline, and Redwin Lewis for their help along the way.

MORE EXCITING NOVELS FROM SHELLEY PEARSALL

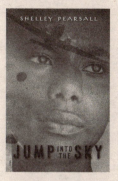

Carrying nothing but a suitcase and a bag of his aunt's good fried chicken, thirteen-year-old Levi Battle heads south to a U.S. Army post in search of his father—a lieutenant in an elite all-black unit of paratroopers. The fact that his father doesn't even know he's coming turns out to be the least of his problems.

★ "[A] poignant, powerful tale of father and son getting to know each other." —*Booklist*, Starred

★ "Levi's voice [is] humorous and acutely insightful." —*The Bulletin*, Starred

Eleven-year-old Samuel was born as Master Hackler's slave, and working the Kentucky farm is the only life he's ever known—until one dark night in 1859. With no warning, cranky old Harrison, a fellow slave, pulls Samuel from his bed. And, together, they run.

"Powerful. . . . A suspenseful, emotional story." —*USA Today*

★ "Action-packed. . . . Gripping from beginning to end." —*Publishers Weekly*, Starred